Lake Conshe

Ingrid Lynch

Lake Conshe

Olympia Publishers
London

www.olympiapublishers.com
OLYMPIA PAPERBACK EDITION

A CIP catalogue record for this title is
available from the British Library.

ISBN: 978-1-80439-251-5

This is a work of fiction.
Names, characters, places and incidents originate from the writer's
imagination. Any resemblance to actual persons, living or dead, is
purely coincidental.

First Published in 2023

Olympia Publishers
Tallis House
2 Tallis Street
London
EC4Y 0AB

Printed in Great Britain

1

When Helen Stedman Robbins arrived at Conshe Mountain, Pennsylvania, in the late fall of 1935, she had no idea she'd be there for the rest of her life. She meant it to be a brief respite, a time of strengthening, and that was all.

She was sitting in a lawn chair at lakeside, admiring the view, glad to be living at the Stedman family's summer cottage on a cool morning. Across the lake were a few visible homes with no hint of the little town beyond them. On this side of the lake where she sat, the entire shoreline was part of the Robbins/Stedman property.

For a while, at least, she was alone, away from her self-important husband and her testy older sister, Eva.

What she thought of as The Cottage was hardly that; the two-story residence had more than four thousand square feet. There were five bedrooms—one downstairs and four on the second floor. There was one full bath on the first floor, four on the second floor, and a large library, also on the second floor. On the first floor, besides the bedroom and bath, there was a huge common room with a fireplace, a dining room, a kitchen, storage space of all sorts, and something called a "butler's pantry" off the kitchen.

The house sat on elevated land that gave it a grand view of the lake and the gardens, and there was a wide, covered front porch. A two-level staircase led from the lawn up to the porch. From where she sat, Helen could see all the way up to the screened front door of the house.

Staff, all local, didn't live in as they had at the house in New York. These workers used the service road at the back of the house every morning and left using it each evening.

Helen, already partially an invalid, would be living on the first floor. Those two strong teens, her son, Sted, and the sturdy helper, Dalt, had pushed her in a wheelchair out to this view. They had moved her to the lawn chair, tucked a light quilt around her, and left her a hand bell she could ring if she needed help.

Sted's full first name, Stedman, was Helen's maiden last name. She'd insisted on giving it to him as a first name because she wanted the world to know her son had her family's noble blood lines. On her closet door hung a coat of arms that was genuine and which meant business. She was often offended by her husband's coarse origins, just as she was comforted by her family's history. She had to share that history with her sister, Eva, a woman so enthralled by the past she had no future, at least not a married one.

All Helen needed at the moment she already had. Eva, who so often visited them, was elsewhere. Her husband, Reginald, was still in New York, meeting with clients and suppliers there. The money for establishing and running their foundry came from Helen's family, but Reginald was the one who knew all the "right people", those who knew all the other "right" people. Reginald made all the connections with those people who, even in hard times, helped the foundry fulfill the railroad's needs. That, of course, made Helen and Reginald and Eva rich. Helen was the one who charted the way financially, even handling the demands of her older sister, who was all about money and little else.

The air today at the lake carried the faint smell of a couple of old horses still kept there at the cottage, and she resolved to solve that. No one rode horses there any more, and it was just an added expense, plus dirt, dust, and smells. She dabbed at her nose with her handkerchief. Dogs and cats—there would be none of those, either.

Already she was looking forward to Christmas in Pennsylvania. There would be friends and family coming from New York. She'd invite a few, a very few, people from Conshe Mountain and nearby. The proper sort, of course. While Sted and her ward, Dalt, would be entering ninth grade the following year at Conshe Mountain High School, attending ninth grade along with the locals on what she hoped would be a temporary basis, their teen friends, if they made any, would have to understand only a few, if any, would ever be invited onto the cottage land, all one hundred fifty up and down acres of it.

Dalt took a photograph of Helen shortly after she arrived at the cottage. It showed a woman who, although physically frail, stood with her head held high, obviously a person of substance and confidence.

Years later, even after her death in early 1944 and her husband's death shortly after, the photograph, brown with age, hung on an entry foyer wall.

But in 1935, when people arrived for a lovely Christmas celebration, the photo, hung by dutiful staff, was fresh and new.

Everyone remembered that lovely time, complete with fires in the huge common room fireplace and a brightly decorated tree in the center of a bay window. There was snow falling, singing, the exchanging of gifts, and plenty of good food. It was a good thing Helen got to enjoy that, for soon after, her health worsened, and then all hell broke loose in the 1940s. The foundry prospered in the war years, but Helen did not.

Stedman Robbins and Dalt Thorson were both born in late 1921 near big population centers—Stedman, near New York

City, and Dalt, near London. What Sted could remember about the house in New York was that it was huge and cold, and the footsteps of staff echoed in it. Dalt's presence in the house came about when Gunnar Thorson was convinced to come to New York to manage the foundry. An extremely handsome man, he might have caused some handkerchief twisting on Helen's part, though she would have denied that. He came to be the very heart and soul of the foundry, for he, his wife, and his son lived in the huge residence with the Robbins's. What Sted could remember about Gunnar was his quiet manner, much different from the clenching and unclenching of his father's fists whenever he was upset, or the biting of his lower lip with his teeth, causing his mustache to twitch. The son, Dalt, was much like his calm father, and the two boys bonded almost at once.

The frightful cold winter of 1933 changed everything. Many families in the city suffered, and the Robbins family was one of them. It was ironic that two of the healthiest people came down with influenza, then pneumonia, and died. Gunnar and Mia, Dalt's parents, had that happen to them. Helen would, in later years, confess to Dalt that she didn't know what else to do, so Dalt stayed on with them. Eva was willing to take the boy in, but Helen wanted to spare him that. Helen herself, so very frail, was affected by the flu, but she seemed to be recovering.

Just when Sted thought his friend would never be the same again, miraculously the foundry and the New York home were left with trusted supervision, and off to Pennsylvania they went, where it was hoped Helen would recover completely.

How delicious the memories were of those first days at the cottage! There were two gentle horses they could ride (till those were sold away), a new residence to explore, a lake to swim, fish and boat in, and miles and miles of grounds and woods. One groundskeeper even had a friendly dog that greeted them with a wagging tail each day. The two tutors who groomed them, getting them ready for ninth grade, were quite pleasant. And so, the following fall, for the first time, the two boys met the public at large and mingled with the common folk.

They thrived on it. True, Helen's health was worse, but the two boys, Sted, with such dark eyes and hair, and Dalt, so blue eyed and fair, blossomed. When asked if they were brothers, they'd laugh and say they were. The rumor began that they both were the sons of the rich man across the lake. Dalt must be the illegitimate son of that man since his last name was different.

By the end of their junior year, they were popular and crass plebeians. They had many friends, chief among them Ricky Halloran, a mouthy representative of the Irish working class in America. There had been so many girlfriends by that time Helen would have been scandalized had she known of it.

But she didn't. The husband, the aunt, and all the staff were so taken up with Helen's health, they let some things slip where the two fellows were concerned. They were even allowed to drive the family Buick around on weekends. Ricky with Gloria; Dalt with the tall blonde Candice, who was called Candy; and Sted with his Faye—what freedom they enjoyed in that car! Life was good. It would continue being good forever.

And then came graduation.

After the graduation ceremony, dinner at the cottage was festive. It was a cool evening, yet the windows near the kitchen were open because the chefs had outdone themselves. Iced crab meat had been bought to make a superb baked crab imperial, and there was also a standing rib roast, along with salads, vegetables, breads, and the favorite dessert, strawberries on shortcake with cream. The two youths, wearing their best pants and shirts with the collars open and the sleeves rolled up, were relaxed and happy. It was Eva who brought up the subject of the future. She knew quite well what the future would hold for Sted. He would be college bound, then take over control of the family's resources. Still, she asked. To hear him say it, one must guess.

"So what do you intend to do next, young master Robbins?" she asked.

If Sted had been thinking, he might have answered differently. But he fell into the trap, as so many graduates do, of thinking his opinion really counted among the adults who provided for him.

A shy smile played over his lips, and he blushed a little. "Well," he said, reaching for his salad fork, "I've fallen in love with a girl named Faye." His eyes shone with the love he felt for her even as he spoke of her. "I'm hoping I can find work and set up housekeeping after we're married."

Silence fell over the table. Eva looked over at her sister Helen, whose eyes were downcast onto her plate. No one in the family had ever heard of a girl named Faye, nor had they heard of any marriage plans, either.

"Indeed," said Eva. By noon the next day, you can be sure Eva knew all there was to be found out about this girl named Faye.

Dalt remembered thinking, along with the rhythm of the beating of his heart, *Big Mistake, big mistake, big mistake.*

Reginald Robbins pushed his chair back and rose from the table. "You and I, Sted, will move to the garden. We'll return in a minute." As his father moved toward the foyer, Sted looked shocked. He slowly put his salad fork down and followed his father.

The two descended to the foot of the stairs leading to the

porch, far enough away that no one, including Eva, could hear them. Reginald's voice was soft, but Sted could sense anger in the man. "Let me tell you a simple truth. You're set to inherit a right smart amount of money someday. At the pleasure of your mother, I must add. Your inheritance is beyond my control, and you can be grateful it's beyond Eva's. Your mother, who loves you, controls that. You'd better be careful not to wipe out her love for you. Or her high opinion of you, for that matter."

Sted stirred, trying to interrupt, to say something, but his father waved his words away. "I'm asking you to listen now. True love waits. That is what it does. If you can't go to college and marry after that, then it was never true in the first place. Your choice is simple: go to college and marry after that and inherit, or marry before anything else and be disinherited and live a life of poverty, your wife included. If you refuse to listen, then you will suffer, as I assure you you will, being cut off from everyone in this family and from all its money."

His father lowered his voice and moved closer to him, making his tone more intimate, more caring. "Sted, you have to meet life on its own terms, as if it were a game of chess, and you must see ahead what may come later on. Think ahead several moves and provide accordingly. Arrangements have already been made for your departure to New York in August. Let's return to the table and announce the postponement of everything else. Be a loving son and agree with what I hope …" he paused, waiting for Sted to speak, to agree.

"Well, Dalt will be coming with me to college, then?"

Reginald was close to losing his temper. "Dalt's been allowed to attend classes with you in spite of the pressure our staff has felt about Helen. Don't be ridiculous. Dalt's needed here to help with moving Helen about and moving equipment."

"You could easily pay someone to attend to whatever duties Dalt would perform," Sted pointed out.

"No one could take Dalt's place in Helen's mind. Her health must include her natural affection for her ward. If you think Dalt expects to go to college with you, you must take him aside and explain to him his responsibilities."

And so, after Reginald's announcement of the change of plans, after the dinner advanced to a silent dessert, the two high school graduates sat together at the bottom of the stairs where the father-son talk had occurred. "I don't know why in the hell they couldn't keep me here and sponsor you, instead, for college. Seems my mother just can't do without you."

"This is just a temporary setback," Dalt said, trying to make things better. "I imagine your mother thinks of your going off to college as if it's a big sacrifice on her part, something she thinks only you can do. I can handle this all right, and you can, too."

"When I have this place, if that ever happens, supposing it will, we'll make this right side up. The two of us, we can do that. You have to hang on here."

"It'll get better. You'll see. Time will pass quickly."

"And it could get worse."

It could get worse, indeed. One must go, who wishes to stay. One must stay, who needs to go.

2

Beauty, around its ruins,
Tendrils of the heart still twine.

Even before he reached the porch, Ricky Halloran was pissed off. He'd called the cottage to tell Dalt and Sted he'd be late for their breakfast together, and they should go ahead and eat. He'd catch up. All he got from Dalt, who answered the phone, were expressive grunts and soft one-syllable words. It always bothered Ricky when he had to talk to Dalt on the phone, and today it bothered him enough that he put a slug of vodka into his morning juice and, later on, another, stronger one after he made some phone calls about the parts he needed for the work he was doing on a classic car in his shop.

Now, as he entered the cottage through the screen door, early this fine June morning in 1987, he slammed that door so hard it made Helen Stedman Robbins's photograph spin around a bit sideways on the foyer wall.

In the kitchen, he announced his presence, "Dalt, you goddamned mummy, we couldn't shut you up in high school, and now you won't talk—"

"He talks when he has to," Sted said defensively from where he was huddled at the kitchen table.

"Like I take a shit when I have to, but how's about, 'Hello, how's it goin'?' when he doesn't have to?"

Dalt, ever the simple chef, was tending to scrambled eggs,

13

back turned, and Ricky, ever the miscreant, emptied the rest of the vodka into the juice pitcher while Sted had his head down, rubbing his forehead. Serve Dalt right, Ricky thought.

Sted looked pale. "I didn't sleep so well last night," he said. "Prowled around. Was there a full moon? Seemed so bright."

Dalt turned. "You all right for fishing?"

"It'll get better."

"Drink a little juice, or have some more coffee. Might help."

Ricky started to say something, then changed his mind. "Guess what's in my shop? Remember the Buick we drove around? I've got one a lot like it … A few parts, and it's good as new. Black, a lot like ours looked. But this one's a Special, an old 38 Special."

Dalt put plates on the table. Ricky and he had the scrambled eggs and a slice of bacon before them. Sted waved it off, not hungry.

Ricky, shorter, louder, and more vulgar than anyone else, had a junkyard, a parts shop, and a car repair shop that some said was a chop shop. (In reality, his mechanics worked hard and liked working for Ricky.) "Wouldn't it be great if I could ever find that same car? Ours? The same car? You think?"

Sted shocked them with what he said next. "I thought I heard Faye singing something last night."

They stared at him, pausing over their food. "He's been having dreams," Dalt was quick to explain.

Ricky put his fork down. "Jesus. We go through World War Two, and he's just fine, and now he's having dreams?"

Reginald Robbins had managed to keep Dalt at the cottage, even in a time of war, using all the connections he had. But he couldn't prevent Sted's volunteering for military service. Miraculously, Sted and Ricky trained together and were 82nd

Airborne, together all during the war. They entered it and came out of it together safely.

"Well, all right, what's she singing?"

"I don't know. But I dreamed she wanted me to know what our boy Bill would have grown up to look like, what he'd be like. You know, look like."

Both Ricky and Dalt were silent hearing that. Faye Livingston was the nicest, most popular girl, exotic and beautiful, yet so friendly everyone loved her. She died when her brother was driving her in his Chevy sedan. A Diamond oil truck lost its brakes, came through an intersection, and hit the sedan broadside, pushing it over a low embankment and retaining wall. The crushed sedan fell about forty feet into a gully.

"You were never sure she was pregnant," Ricky said softly.

"Heading to a doctor's appointment, maybe," Dalt whispered.

Ricky shrugged, "Let's get outta here and go catch some fish!" He had his gear out on the porch, and he was wearing his fishing hat with a few lures tied onto it.

Last out, he slammed the screen door again so hard the photograph of Helen Stedman Robbins flipped back into its original position.

"Stop this about Faye. That's no good. Let's talk about Dalt and Candice instead! Woo woo! Whatta chick. Oh, my Candice, my sweet Candy! I wuv you so! Will you sleep with me?"

Dalt turned, threatening him. "I'll conk you on the head so hard your eyes will fall out! You shut up!"

They stomped across the porch and then came to an abrupt halt. Even from where they stood, they had a view of the lake, and they could see, in the distance, a man fishing. He wore a brown looked-like-plaid shirt and a casual fishing hat. As they watched, his fishing line flicked right to a high spot behind him, stayed suspended there for a half split second, and then, as he snapped a sharp wrist movement, swooped forward and landed exactly where these three oldsters would have put it—out where an underwater ledge was favored by lake trout who hung out under it.

"That fellow's usin' my good spot," Ricky muttered. "I think he knows this lake pretty good."

Sted never cared about people fishing along the lake front. It was fine with him. "Ricky, he can fish where he wants."

Ricky was lighting a cigar.

"Oh, here we go again with a stinkin' cigar," Dalt mourned.

"Let's go see him," Ricky said, armed as he was with his gear and his cigar. "Let's move on."

They muddled across the lawn to the unsuspecting fisherman who was wearing waders in the water up to his hips. Sted trailed a little behind.

"Hey, there," Ricky hailed him. "Catchin' anything?"

"Not yet. Might have waited too long to get out here. It's all right for me to fish here? I've heard so."

"It's okay."

The fisherman turned toward them. He looked to be in his forties. His eyes were dark, like Sted's, and he had curly dark hair peeking out from his fishing hat. His smile was open and friendly.

"I'm Bill—" he was about to add his last name, but the noise made by Sted falling down flat with a surprised expression on his face interrupted the introduction.

"What the fuck!" came Ricky's exclamation.

The fisherman standing in the water jumped fearfully away from them.

"It's all right," Dalt said to him. "He's not feeling well. We'll

16

take care of him. Keep on fishing."

"Can I help you any?" the surprised fisherman asked.

"No!" Ricky announced. With some difficulty, they got Sted to a spot on the lawn where there were a few rustic chairs, and once they saw Sted didn't need a doctor, at least not for that moment, they helped him to his feet.

"I can't believe I did that!" Sted fumed. "What the hell happened?"

He ascended the porch stairs with them on each side. In the kitchen he dropped into a rocker Dalt usually sat in to read a newspaper. "I'm sorry. He took me by surprise."

"What the hell does that mean?" Ricky was winded. He sat down at the kitchen table, his fishing hat a bit sideways.

"Bill. His name's Bill. Faye and I, we said our baby would be Bill, a boy—"

Ricky drew a long breath. "Here we go."

Dalt was thoughtful. "I think I'll make some coffee. Ricky, it's more than that. I'm going to tell him what's been going on with you, Sted."

Sted protested by weakly throwing up his hands.

"Sometimes, when he's alone, he looks into the dining room, and he thinks he sees Faye, like a ghost figure, sitting at the table. She's not moving or anything, but he also sees a little boy sitting there on the other side of the table, and he seems real. He changes, sometimes one age, sometimes another."

"This fishing guy. He looks about the right age. He's old enough to be my son." Sted was shaken.

"Goddamn it, Sted, he's not your son!" Ricky exclaimed.

"I know that! But Faye said I could see what he'd be like grown up… I thought …"

"Faye never said anything, dammit."

17

Dalt turned from where he stood at the kitchen counter. "There're those two pocket doors that close off the dining room from the great room. I'm keeping them closed now, except when Nell and Tim are here. Out of sight, out of mind. Could help."

"I think I'll go lie down for a while." Sted made his way toward the downstairs bedroom.

When Sted had returned to the cottage after the war, Dalt took the upstairs as his own, and Sted had taken the downstairs.

When Nell Lawson came during the week, they enjoyed her cooking, but usually it was Dalt who came downstairs to cook. Nell came twice a week to clean and cook. The last time Nell was there, she had looked at the closed pocket doors to the dining room suspiciously. "What's goin' on back there?" she asked. Dalt had hurried to open them.

Nell Lawson was a woman of color and courage. Her younger son, Tim, came with her to help in the garden. There was no other staff these days.

"Ricky, he keeps saying he should have been driving that car."

"This is nuts. He needs help from somebody. If you think of how I can help, I will, if you just ask me. I'm goin' back to the shop. I'll call you later on to see how he's doin'. Try to talk to me with more than just two fuckin' words, okay?"

"Ricky, if you could just use some other adjective—"

The slamming of the door cut off the end of Dalt's sentence.

After Ricky left, Sted called to Dalt from his bedroom. "I wish you hadn't told him all that. Now he thinks I'm crazy."

Dalt took some of his freshly made coffee—which nobody drank—out onto the porch after he made sure Sted was asleep.

June was glorious in the garden. Dalt could see that from where he sat in a wicker rocker. There were peony bushes, like the old red and white Circus Maximus, perfuming the air, some so big at the roots they were bushel basket size; they'd been in the garden for that many years. There were oriental lilies, day lilies, Shasta daisies, and against one side of the garden, a tall hedge of lilacs. Pathways were lined with iris, and a corner was crowded full of hollyhocks. There was at least an acre full of plants that were either coming into bloom, were in full bloom, or were ending bloom. That wasn't even counting the one huge area given over entirely to rose bushes.

Dalt remembered something Helen had said about the garden. She was losing her balance then. He caught her and helped her back into her wheelchair. "I hate being a bother like this," she said.

"You're not a bother," he tried to reassure her. What was a bother was the fact that back in those days nobody heard from Sted. After the awful argument about Faye's death, when Sted came home from college just before Christmas, once he went to war, it was as if he turned his back on his parents and Dalt. They depended on Ricky's parents and his girlfriend to give them news of Sted. It was as if Helen took the place of the mother he lost, and he, Dalt, took the place of the son she never heard from.

"At least, you and I, we're in one beautiful spot," she said. When she said that, she was just months away from her death. To make matters worse, the old gentleman, Reginald, was beginning to crumble.

"I couldn't find any family in Britain for you, and I had no idea about Scandinavia," Helen told Dalt. "I couldn't stand the idea of an orphanage or of Eva's household, so being with us and Sted seemed natural. I'm proud of you and Sted, though I guess he doesn't think so. But when we look outside in June, Dalt, doesn't beauty still reign here? Isn't it glorious?"

19

Do houses hang onto things, Dalt wondered, *and hold grudges, making us see and hear things that were once and are no more? When the atmosphere is just right, do those footsteps on the stairs repeat those of years ago because the house chooses to release them so we hear them? Was Sted,* he wondered, *a victim of a house determined to make him see the past again?*

In another way, the house was a problem for Dalt, and so were the foundry and the house in New York. The war ended close enough to the funerals of Helen and Reginald that the very existence of their son came into question. Stedman Lewis Robbins was beginning to be thought of as dead. At the parents' funerals, Eva advised Dalt to start packing.

Terrified, Dalt contacted a lawyer. In turn, the lawyer contacted the senators and representatives of Pennsylvania, who got in touch with the Pentagon, who found Sted, whether he wanted to be found or not. There finally came a phone call. When Sted realized Eva was about to take over everything, he appeared with lawyers and restraining orders and court actions that made it possible for Dalt to pay the bills and continue to keep the cottage running from day to day.

It was Lela Sterling who came into the cottage to help straighten out the bill paying, the catch-up work for unpaid taxes, and the estimating of what could be afforded in the future and what could not. Dalt found out from Lela that Sted had provided a pension for him, so that no matter what happened, he would have an income. It made him feel like an unschooled child, learning things from her, a young and attractive woman.

He also learned there was a new will, one that put on Sted the responsibility for all things for so long as he lived or until he was incapacitated. If Sted became so ill he couldn't function, or if he were declared insane, he, Dalt, would inherit the whole mess, with all its benefits and problems. He knew some people had murdered for less.

In the 1950s and 1960s, and even after, the family millions were intact. The war had been profitable. Sted simplified things. He sold the New York home, and in the 1950s the foundry was sold. The bank, which had been threatening to foreclose on the cottage was now politely silent. Eva had to leave the New York home.

Things were looking fine for Dalt now in 1987. Yet, he sat in the wicker chair, clutching his coffee mug, and he wept. He wept because it wasn't just Ricky who was doubting Sted's sanity. Dalt himself was noticing ways Sted no longer seemed to care about anything. He remembered Sted sitting near the Christmas tree that fateful Christmas, staring out into the woods, and he wondered if reality wasn't slipping away from Sted even then, when Faye's death had just happened.

Nothing must challenge Dalt's loyalty to Sted. Dalt owed too much to him. He couldn't doubt Sted's goodness or his sanity, not ever.

He and Ricky discussed that, in a sense, long before they knew there was a problem. Ricky told many a tale about how he saved Sted from acts of carelessness. "Didn't you see some men who seemed to have charmed lives?" Dalt asked Ricky.

Ricky allowed there were such men; yes, there were. Men who should have been dead but weren't because of some strange luck that seemed to be perched on their shoulders.

"Then, maybe, because you were near him and his strange luck, maybe that's why you're alive today. Maybe being near him saved you."

Ricky was unimpressed. He grinned. "Fuck you," he said.

While Sted, who had been so haunted at night, slept during

the daylight hours, Dalt rocked a little on the porch, begging God, begging the house itself, to show mercy on his friend, his brother.

Spread out before him; the garden comforted him. Helen was right. They lived surrounded by beauty.

3

Candy dandy
Liquor quicker

Now it was a slow-poke late June morning, hazy, promising to be hot. Sted was on the porch relaxing when Dalt came out.

"Marilyn's sleeping in," Dalt said.

"Fine. But Nell and Tim will be here tomorrow. You want to meet her somewhere else for anything overnight? Or put it off."

Dalt nodded in agreement. He entertained whenever he wanted to, including overnight women.

"Is Marilyn a serious thing?"

Dalt shrugged. "Ricky called. He says he's coming to pick you up, go to the diner."

Sted hadn't heard from Ricky since the incident at the lake.

"He says word around town is that you're sick and you need to be seen in public or they'll have you dead. Also, he says he's got some information about that fisherman, and he wants you to hear it."

"That stuff about me. How'd that get started?"

"Well, the fisherman probably said something to Nell about you falling down. He's boarding at her house now."

"Nell has room for a boarder? Did her mother die?"

"Not that I know of. But her older son Tom has moved out of the house, and that's a good thing. He's not much good. Maybe that's how she has room. Anyway, Ricky probably got information from Gloria because she has Nell cleaning at their place pretty regularly."

When Dalt wanted to cook for a guest, especially if it were a woman guest, Sted ate elsewhere. Usually this would be with Ricky at the truck stop diner. Their eating system had worked for the two men for years. And the cooking at the diner was pretty good. Not as good as Nell's, but a little better than Dalt's.

At the diner, Ricky was friendly. "I guess that vodka screwed us up," he said. Sted locked eyes with him, and Ricky's face flushed. He looked away. "Well, then, let's move on," he said.

Ricky's words brought a memory to Sted, a war moment when the glider they were in was having a problem. A tiny hole in that canvas bottom was getting bigger and bigger as the glider kept going on. When they finally landed, they all piled out, led by their officers, and within a few minutes the two officers were dead, picked off by snipers.

"Get away from the glider! Move it!" That was runty Ricky taking charge. Over their shoulders, Sted and Ricky saw the kid from Wisconsin, Mac, standing still as if confused by the tiny spurts of dirt kicking up. No sound, just little fountains of dirt, which made him stop and stare.

"Mac! Snipers! It ain't no chipmunks! Get over here! C'mon!" They all huddled behind some scant cover away from the glider, slightly behind it.

"We're behind the goddamned German lines," Ricky said sorrowfully.

"What makes you so sure of that?" Sted was instantly sorry he asked that. Ricky fixed him with a sarcastic eye that said without words, *idiot*. "Who the fuck do you think is shootin' at us, Sted?" he asked.

It was Ricky who analyzed their every move. Any high point, a steeple, a cliff or hill, if it overlooked an open area meant that in daylight, they must not cross. Why? Because if it was us, that's what we'd do if it were the other way around. So Ricky had them moving mostly at night. And when he was sure of what he was doing, that's what he always said: "Let's move on, then." When Sted heard him say it again, it put him back into the war for a moment.

Even in darkness, you could make mistakes. Sted was about to step around a hedgerow onto a narrow road when Ricky stopped him. "Boots," he whispered. They lay still till the German patrol had passed.

It was good the diner was crowded and full of life. It helped keep Sted grounded with where he was, who he was, and what year it was. The truck drivers ate and rolled out, so service was quick and the food was good. "Yes, move on," Sted said.

"Nell told Gloria some stuff she knows about her boarder, and you need to know this, Sted." Ricky had some things written down on a sheet of paper. "He's a teacher! Can you imagine that? A teacher can flex a line out like that? Oh, well… anyway, his parents are retired air force, and they're alive, and they live out west. His last name is Accardi. Bill Accardi. Now, listen to this. His dad is from an Italian family. That's where he gets that curly, black hair. And probably that big smile, too. Italian. You got that, Sted? He can't be your son. He's got real live parents."

Ricky was looking at him closely now. Sted nodded in agreement. "Yes, I see that," he said. Ricky looked relieved.

"Nell said he's single. Was married but got divorced. So it's all normal, huh?"

"Sounds just fine."

"There's more. Tim knows this teacher. He told Nell there's this kid in the junior high named Jimmy Stevens, and he's such a bad number he wanders around the building wherever he wants to. He's even been throwing lit firecrackers into classrooms."

Sted's eyes widened. "Shouldn't be there, then."

"Yeah. Well, they don't expel kids like they used to, Sted, when we were there. And this boy's uncle, his mother's brother, is Frank Wilkes, chairman of the school board. So that has something to do with it, I guess, too. You remember how the junior high and the high school is all connected together, right? We were all in the old part, and that's where this Bill teacher is, see. Anyway, the Stevens kid chased some little sixth grader into the high school part, and he's got him down on the floor, kicking the crap out of him. Bill, he must have heard something, he opens his door, sees what's going on, and he pulls the Stevens kid off the little guy by the hair of his head. I love this part. He drags the Stevens kid into his classroom by his hair, throws him into a closet, and then he locks it! I'm lovin' this guy. He tells the class to be quiet while he takes the little guy to the nurse, and then here he comes back with an administrator. They unlock the closet and get the Stevens kid out. Here's a good part: the Stevens kid is yelling threats at the teacher when he's on the way out. Tim says the teacher almost lost his job over that, but he's popular, so he didn't. This Bill teacher, he doesn't get rattled easy."

Sted's eyes were wide, taking all this information in. "You're full of knowledge this evening, Ricky," he said softly.

"There's something else," Ricky said, as if it might be urgent.

"Can hardly wait."

"Fellows talk, and my mechanics picked up some talk from high schoolers who got it from middle schoolers. It concerns your

26

place, Sted."

"My place?"

"This Stevens kid, he's saying he prowls around your place just about every night. He says nobody to stop him, so he can go wherever he wants to, do what he wants to."

"Just talk?"

"I don't think so. Because the fellows at the shop say the kid is saying he's seen Dalt on the second floor with women, not always the same woman, and he's saying he's seen you sleep on the first floor in the room that has lots of windows in it. That sort of set me back because it sounds as if that's what he's seein'."

Sted sat quietly, saying nothing.

"What you going to do?"

"I don't really know. It isn't all that serious, at least not yet, now is it? Try to catch him at it, I guess." He took a long sip of his drink. "You got on Dalt's nerves about the Candice gal; you know that, changing the subject. Want to know why?"

Ricky raised an eyebrow. "Sure." Ricky was in a comfortable mood. He'd just eaten, and anything about Dalt was fair game.

"While the two of us were freezing our asses off in Europe in a war, Dalt married her."

"Never heard about that. Why didn't we know about that?"

"It'll be clear in a minute. My mother gave Dalt a thousand dollars so he could have a honeymoon with her. Now, you know how fussy she was, but she did that; imagine that. So Dalt, he calls up this lodge, and he makes a reservation for a week. He figures there's fine dinners, long walks, romantic baths, the works. But as they're driving along, Miss Candice says she doesn't want to go to any fancy lodge, soon as she finds out where they're going. She'd rather be at some bar where there's lots of people having fun, she says. So Dalt, he has to call up the lodge and cancel, and then when they get to a town, he sees this pretty little hotel, and he says they could stay there. Nah, she says somebody might see them."

"Are you making this up?"

"It's true, I'm telling you. Well, Dalt, he drives till he comes to a motel, and he says to her, 'This is it. I'm tired.' She says, 'Only if we get twin beds.' So in he goes, gets the room. When he suggests they could push the beds together, she says, 'No, somebody might hear us.' When he wakes up, she's not even in the same room with him. She's over on a park bench across the street in a park or someplace like that. Dalt, he packs up, and he swings the car over there and picks her up, says, 'Get in,' and she does. He drives her back to the cottage, them not talking much, and she clomps up the stairs to the quarters mother has fixed for them. Mother takes a look at Dalt's face, and I guess she saw how things went. She says for Dalt to come in where she is, and she fixes up a pitcher of lemonade that is loaded with vodka and other stuff, maybe even some sleeping pills crushed up, who knows."

"Your mother… we thinking of the same woman?"

"Well, it worked, and Dalt got the job done by next morning. But he wasn't happy by a long shot. He always figured he'd have a willing participant, at least not somebody who was snoring. Anyway, the spiked lemonade trick got used a lot, and Candice decided she liked it. Any time she wanted some action, she started following Dalt around, and the staff could hear what she said to him, which was this: 'Let's have a drinkey-poo, so we can have some pokey-poke.' Worse, sometimes she'd come up behind him, and, Ricky, I know you can remember how long-legged that girl was—"

"Jesus, God, Yes."

28

"Well, she'd plant her belly on his ass, and then drape one leg around his legs, and then, she'd take an arm and reach around him and go patty cake on his crotch and say that little 'Let's have a drinkey-poo' stuff. So, one day it's not just the staff working there get a load of what's happening to Dalt, it's Eva who's hearing it, and she goes to Helen and says, 'Helen, is that repulsive woman saying what I think she's saying?' Mother tells Dalt he should let Candice go visit her family during the week and just stay at the cottage on weekends, and finally that marriage died out because she just stayed away for good at the end."

Ricky was skeptical. "Dalt will kill you if he ever finds out you told this."

"I figure you'll lay off the subject now you know. Thank your lucky stars you have a normal marriage. You got lucky. Dalt and me, where marriage is concerned, we got screwed."

Ricky was looking down into his cup. "You two poor bastards," he said.

Back at the cottage, Sted told Dalt what he'd learned about their prowler. Dalt was surprised. "There's not much we leave out on the grounds, but I think he must have been in the garage, then. I was sure I left my leather gloves in the car, and they're gone. And in the hay room, I could tell some hay was strewn around. It looked as if somebody decided to make himself comfortable there. I told myself it was just from the hay being there for so long, you know, but now, well, it could be something else. In the garden sheds, too, maybe a lot of things were moved around, left disturbed. Now, it bothers me. What's to be done?"

"Don't know. So far, it's not too serious. We'll think of something."

What had once been stables, was now a long garage, in

which they kept an old pick-up that still did the job and a fairly new car. There was still a tack room that had a shower and toilet attached. The hay room was all that was left of a barn.

Dalt was standing at the side of the lake while they talked.

"Looking to see if any fish are jumping?" Sted asked.

"Nah, too hot. They're in the middle of the lake now, I think, where it's cooler."

"Yes," Sted said, "where the lake is deepest." As he walked away, he thought to himself, the little bastard had been in the hay room, too.

The hay room was where he took her virginity, and she took his. They pledged themselves to each other. The words "forever and ever" were spoken there so many times by those two lovers he was surprised that when he looked into that room, he couldn't hear those words rattling around there yet. By lantern light, they joined together in the hay. By the time he left for college in August, they felt themselves to be a married couple, pledged to each other, to be true forever and ever. Was she pregnant? He felt damn right she was.

And he couldn't even have that much. A simple hay room left undefiled. Faye would have been such a grand daughter-in-law, such a loving wife, if only she had been given a chance.

The prowler could wait. Sted felt sure he could deal with a prowler. All in good time.

4

Casserole, Crayons
All you need

Sted had bad dreams as a child. He remembered dreams that held a sense of falling from great heights. One, in particular, had angels pulling his crib up and away and then releasing it. In another, he stood on a tower and fell off. He always startled awake before he hit the ground.

Somehow, the scrawny kid with the dreams of falling had become a man, and those dreams disappeared. After the war, he sometimes had depressing dreams in which he was looking for his family, feeling lost, and wandering in strange surroundings that had some familiar elements but never enough.

This new dream was different because it filled him with such rage it woke him up. He dreamed he saw a little fellow, a toddler, being chased by a much larger kid. He knew at once this was his little boy, Bill, the child Faye should have had. The little one was on the ground, screaming, with the big child kicking him. It made Sted so angry he woke up. The child's wailing was fresh in his mind as he sat up and struggled out of bed.

There is nothing like being older, waking up, thinking it must be midnight, or close to dawn, and seeing it's only ten or eleven o'clock at night. Once he saw that was the case, Sted wandered into the kitchen, thinking he might as well make himself some coffee or tea since he was awake anyway. He decided to sit in the big rocker Dalt favored so much. He rocked in it, rubbing his eyes.

He became aware, then, of someone humming a melody, and, as he listened, he heard lullaby words:

"Jesus loves us, this we know ..."

It became quicker and louder, and it changed. He'd heard Faye sing, and now he became a little afraid, for he knew it was her voice singing. Her voice once thrilled his soul to the core.

"Jesus loves the little children;

Yes, he loves us everyone.

Red and yellow, black and white,

We are precious in his sight;

Jesus loves ..."

It came from the direction of the common room and the dining room. He rose from the rocker and headed in that direction.

There was a faint glow in the dining room. He rounded the corner and saw the pocket doors were open. Dalt had left them open because Nell and Tim would be coming to work the next morning. Inside, seated at the table, he wasn't surprised to see a translucent likeness of Faye sitting silently, just as he'd seen her before. He could see through her, and she looked straight ahead, not acknowledging him in any way, or perhaps, being so unreal, she was unaware he was even there. She was unmoving, not frightening.

What gladdened his heart immediately was the little boy who sat in a chair opposite her. He was happily real, solid, and moving. His baby face broke into a smile, and he raised his arms, wiggling in his chair, begging to be picked up.

"Daddy!" he exclaimed.

Sted reached behind, feeling for the pocket doors and closed them behind himself.

Next morning, when Dalt came downstairs, he saw the dining room pocket doors were closed. When he opened them, he found Sted seated at the table, his head down upon it. He was fast asleep.

Bill Accardi and Tim Lawson were up early, crack of dawn. In a few hours, Nell and Tim would be reporting for the usual Wednesday/Thursday work at the cottage, but, for now, these two fellows wanted a brief try at catching some fish on Sted's side of the lake. Nell's boat, with its silly little motor, was taking them to the cottage dock.

As they got closer, Bill could see someone was on the porch at the cottage, someone whose head popped up attentively as they approached, someone now standing, putting a fishing hat on its head, and hastily gathering up its rod and gear. That person headed for the steps, hurried down them and stumped on short legs toward the lake.

"Is that Sted?" Bill asked Tim.

"No, that's Mister Ricky. My cousin works for him. He likes to fish."

"Cut the motor. We'll drift in to the dock. That'll give him time to get to us. Does he have a favorite spot here?"

But Ricky had already arrived at that spot, close to the dock, where he put down his gear and planted his feet possessively.

"He was probably sittin' there waitin' for the other two to come out and fish. He leaves his gear on that porch all the time," Tim explained.

Bill greeted him. "We meet again. Is it all right if we fish a little bit, an hour or less, far away from you, up there a bit?"

"Sure. You're plenty early."

"Fish I hope are early, too. I'd like a trout."

Ricky gave a short, polite laugh. But there was no laughing on Ricky's part when, just a short time later, he realized that Bill, standing where he was in the shallows, had caught a fish in less than ten minutes from the moment he arrived there. A few minutes later, Bill caught another one.

Possibly Ricky didn't realize how sound travels on a still morning over water. "Sumbitch. What's he using, anyway?" Ricky was looking through his gear at his lures.

Tim answered. "Mr. Ricky, it looks like a little fish with a skirt on."

Ricky's head came up, caught by the description of that. "Huh?"

"He's probably got one. He just forgot it," Bill murmured. To Ricky he called out, "It's a French spinner. I'm sending you one." Ricky's head came straight up hearing that. Tim was sent over to him with the lure.

"Rocky places," Bill called to him, continuing. "I like to use it here where there's lots of rocks. Trout go for it, and sometimes bass. Small mouth."

"Uh *huh*," said Ricky. Even though they moved farther away from him, they heard him exclaim and knew he'd caught a fish.

"He's at Sted's place a lot," said Tim. "I bet you never fish alone from now on. When he sees you fishing, that is."

"Fine with me. I don't mind company when I fish. If a man likes to fish, he's a person who means you no harm." Nell would like the two fish they had for her.

Nell Lawson could read body language and figure people out pretty well. Bill Accardi, she figured, loved two things. He loved teaching, and he loved fishing.

Some people didn't like a white man, like Bill, living at a

black woman's home. That would include her older son Tom. When he stopped by, his dark face showed his disapproval. Nell knew Bill was attracted to this big old house of hers perched right on the water, with its little skiff that could take him to every corner of this lake, and the lake itself, known for its fine fishing. There could be a family of lepers living in her house and Bill would have tried to fit in, just so he could fish.

She liked Bill. She watched him when Tom stopped by, glowering. Bill looked at Tom, sized him up as trouble, but wasn't afraid of him. He wouldn't provoke Tom, so Bill wasn't going to be a problem, no trouble maker.

Nell knew about troubles. Her aged mother lived with them, and that was both a good and a bad thing. Nell spent a lot of time helping her.

Earlier in her life, Nell married a huge black man who deserted her and the little boy, Tom. It was hard being a black boy with no father, and drugs came to fill that void. Later on, she tried again, this time with a man of Spanish origin, but when she wouldn't marry him, he lost interest. Tim was her son by that man. So much for men, then. Fortunately, Tim was a good son, one she was proud of.

When Tom began fighting with his lighter-skinned, bookish younger brother, Nell finally got tough with him and insisted he move out and live somewhere else. He was still her son, and she still loved him, but she knew he sold drugs, and she didn't like it.

On Wednesdays and Thursdays, Nell and Tim worked at the cottage. Nell cleaned and cooked, and Tim worked outside in the garden. For those two days, Sted and Dalt enjoyed a cleaner house and better cooking. Except for landscapers, there weren't any others working at the cottage any more. It took two days for Nell to clean the cottage, but she didn't mind that, for each room was impressive.

In winter and in bad weather, Nell and Tim traveled by car, but in summer, when it was calm and fair, they came across the lake in the little boat, enjoying the trip back and forth. Sometimes Tim would stay overnight, ready to work on Thursday, and he ate with the men.

Nell always wore an outfit that somehow reminded her of a uniform, despite Sted telling her she didn't need to, that she could wear any old thing. She ate at five, so she could get back to her house in plenty of time to cook a meal for her mother. From the porch of the cottage, she could see her house, right at the edge of the lake, a place she was so proud of, knowing, as she did, how many Realtors and white people wanted to have her place.

What made her strong was her sympathy for the two men who lived together at this "cottage", this place that had once been so proud, her love for her mother and her two sons, and her admiration for the teacher living under her roof. She heard the stories people told, those who had worked at the cottage, about how unbending and rigid the owners once were; those women, in particular, who lived here once. Some tried to convince the woman Helen to let those poor old tired horses live out their final years where they were. She wouldn't hear of it. In her heart, Nell knew Sted Robbins always had a mother, but he never had a mamma.

She felt his pain and sorrow about his lost love, Faye. Everyone knew Faye was as much black as she was white, but she was so beautiful and so friendly, everyone put that aside. Her dark hair hung down her back, and everybody said, "Now, see, that's the Spanish in her," glossing over her half-black family, her black neighborhood, and all of that.

And that child could sing. Nell remembered one Mother's Day at church, Faye sang a song about a mother Nell had never heard before. She still remembered when Faye sang this line: "Now I teach my children each melodious measure." The sun streamed in through a window behind Faye and lit her up, so that some in the congregation gasped and some cried. That voice didn't come from any Spaniards, Nell knew. That singing voice came from being partly black.

She and Tim arrived early, and they stepped out onto the cottage dock. Nell never missed anything new, and now her attention was drawn to a tarp or tarps folded neatly with two small anchors on top of them. "What's that about?" she asked Sted, who was at the dock when they arrived.

"Our boat needs caulking. If we get a hard rain, I'll come out and cover it so it doesn't sink. And we always have anchors get snarled up on snags on the bottom of the lake. It's just temporary."

Nell lost interest at once. "Did you remember to get napkins? Paper napkins?" she asked. When Sted looked blank, she added, "Never mind, I brought some."

Tim followed her into the kitchen with the things she always brought. But when he crossed the porch on his way to the garden, Sted stopped him.

"Keep an eye out for Dalt's leather gloves, will you? He's lost them someplace. Tim, what size feet you got there?"

"What?"

"What size are your feet? Your shoes. I might get you some zippy new athletic shoes. First, though, you have to look for something for me."

"Eleven and a half. Yeah, pretty big. What, besides the gloves."

"You know where that dry creek is?" Sted was referring to a creek that carried water every spring, but then in June soon ran dry, becoming just another place where it was hard to walk with too many loose rocks.

"Yeah, sure."

"I found a rock there one time. Can't find it any more. If you find it or a rock that's like it, I'll pay you extra and get you those shoes, and you will go put that rock on the window sill in the hay room. It's large, a little bigger than a person's heart, and it's heart-shaped. Don't worry, the weeds can wait."

Tim found himself standing on the dry creek bed, looking at hundreds of rocks that were lying about, wondering which rock would have a snake beneath it.

Sted joined Dalt on the porch. He took the rocker next to Dalt's and accepted the iced tea offered to him. "I looked in the hay room," Sted began, "and I think you're right. The little bastard was in there. I could kill him for that."

"Then we'd better take that old lantern out of there," Dalt said. "He could start a fire with it if he wanted to."

"I noticed your friend Marilyn parked her car back there on the service road. If that kid is coming up that service road to get to us, she'd be better off to park out in front. We should lock up the car and the pick-up, and the garage and the sheds, too, for that matter. He's never been in the house, evidently, but you never know."

Dalt said thoughtfully, "Did you mean that about killing him?"

"Did I say that? I do still have that Colt 38, come to think of it. I guess I could sneak up behind him and fire some shots in the air and scare the piss out of him. It doesn't seem all that serious a thing, right? We'll think of something to let him know we know he's here. Think on it a while."

They rocked awhile in agreeable silence. Then, Sted added, "That hay room was where I made love to Faye. Damn right it makes me mad when he claims it as his little nap room."

Dalt asked softly, "After Faye, have you ever been in bed with anybody at all?"

"No."

There was silence for a bit. Dalt spoke up, finally. "Marilyn, she's history. She has no sense of humor."

"Well, I hear from others that once we marry, our wives think nothing we say is serious anyway, and we're all just clowns without makeup."

"Pitiful."

"I hope we have one of Nell's casseroles for dinner."

Later, the two men, satisfied and happy after her cooking, were once again sitting together on the porch when Nell came out to leave.

Nell had the second floor to do the following day. It took her all of Wednesday to finish the first floor. As she was leaving, she handed Dalt a sheet of paper she'd found on the dining room floor.

"Were there any children visiting?" she asked. "I found some of their art work on the dining room floor."

Dalt felt the hairs on the back of his neck and his arms rising. The childish drawing showed two stick figures, one much taller, perhaps an adult, and one smaller, perhaps a child, walking together under a big yellow sun. There were smiles on the circle faces. The drawing was done all in crayon.

So far as he knew, there were no crayons in the house.

When he showed it to Sted, Sted shook his head. He said he'd never seen it and had no idea where it came from. Dalt studied his friend's face. It seemed to Dalt Sted was telling the truth.

5

He wouldn't hurt a fly

When Bill Accardi stood lakeside at Nell's house, across the lake on the opposite shore, he could see two white pointed objects rising above the greenery. But when he fished on that side of the lake, he saw nothing of the sort.

Today, as he looked at those puzzling objects again, he could sense Nell was at her kitchen sink, moving around where a window was open, facing in that direction.

"Nell," he called, "can you see those two white points over there at that house?" He didn't yet refer to Sted's home as the *cottage*. "What are those things?"

"They're angel wings," came the answer.

"What?"

"They're the tips, the tops, the angel statue wings, where Faye's body is buried."

"Faye? Who?"

Bill was doubtful about a body buried on that property, based on what he'd heard about the previous owners.

Nell appeared from the kitchen side door. "After Sted got back from the war, him and Ricky. After Sted's parents died. He asked her family if he could move her there, and they said yes. He loved her, but she died." Nell stood looking across the lake, still wearing her apron.

"Those two men, they're not a homosexual couple?"

"Oh, no."

"I've heard Sted is rich."

"I suppose so. Maybe not as much as before."

"Do they travel, or gamble, or run women, or anything like that?"

"No, none of that. Not that I know of."

"They live there, and they fish."

"More to them than that." Nell defended them. "Sted does a lot of good. He's just quiet about it. Just some people know. He went into the army, him and his friend, it was either when he was there or before he finished college, to fight in the war. You got to know him, you'd like him, and he'd want you to have supper with them. Women go after Dalt. He's been interested in more than a few. But Sted, no."

Bill looked across the lake, thinking a huge angel statue over the grave of a lost love was pure Hollywood. But it was good to know, and an angel was a good thing. Good to have an angel nearby, even a giant one. After his divorce, he agreed with the poem that said *Men have died, and worms have eaten them, but not for love.* It was hard to understand a man so devoted to someone who was dead. But then, it was hard for Bill, these days, to understand devotion to a living woman, much less a dead one. Sted was a puzzlement.

Sometimes, the unexpected comes on a drowsy Sunday afternoon. Nell, after church, was watching television. Tim had gone off with friends, and Bill was nodding over a sports equipment catalog when Sted arrived at Nell's door. He was carrying a large, heavy book.

"Let me get this to that table, please," he said, "and let me know what you think of this."

The Expedition of Lewis and Clark was the book's title. Bill looked at it with astonishment. The book's leather binding was cracked and torn, but intact. The book's pages were still attached to its spine, but they were fragile, coming away in small pieces at his touch. It appeared to be old, but its huge size worked against it.

"I teach history, Mr. Sted—"

"Please call me Sted, like everybody—"

"… but I'm no expert about books. This book looks to be old, and I'm thinking you shouldn't be taking it around. You're better off keeping it in one place, probably. It could be valuable, so you need to get an expert, somebody who really knows about books. Why bring it over here to me?"

"Could I sit down?" Sted asked, already seating himself at Nell's dining table.

Bill looked at Nell. She nodded. "Well, yes—"

"See, the problem is like this. Dalt has the upstairs at the cottage. He likes to entertain. I don't, so I have the downstairs. The biggest room on the second floor is the library. It has a big fireplace and lots of space, and Dalt wants to take down all those shelves, repair the walls, and paint, and then he'll have a fine living room. It sounds so simple, but it's not. That library is shelves floor to ceiling on all sides, hundreds of books. And it's not just the library. There's books all over the place, upstairs and down. Let's take British naval history, for example, for there's so many of those; might be a book on that on one side of the room, others scattered all over the place on other sides of the room.

"Nobody has ever collected the books according to their subject, so they're all over the place in a jumble. So, Dalt and I agree now's the time to get the books organized, collect them in piles in the common room, according to subject, and then, when that's done, call in some expert to look at them. So many of them are old. Maybe all of them are. God knows. There's no school now, so I got thinking you could help us. It would be you, me, Dalt, and I hope Lela, too, getting them organized, and I will pay everybody well to do it. Then, Lela has connections in the antique world, so she could put us in touch with somebody to evaluate the whole thing. We could even do some fishing before we go to work most days, what do you think? When we got done, maybe each person could keep a book of his or her own, to collect, or as an investment? For the fun of it?"

"Well, you still need an expert to come in over there—"

"Certainly, once we got the books in the right order. What do you think? The pay would be good."

Sted smiled, trying to be charming.

Bill sat down at the table across from Sted. He looked uncertain. "Mind if I speak plainly?" he asked.

Sted crossed his arms and leaned back in the chair, smiling. "Go right ahead."

He was obviously pleased to hear Bill speak. That was clear.

"I've been fishing with Ricky a few times lately. I'm not any kind of reincarnation of your son. I'm not someone who is what your son would have been if he lived. I'm not even someone who looks like your son would have looked. Ricky says you understand that now. But if anything came up about that, and it bothered me, I'd have to walk right out on you. You understand that?"

For a minute, Sted's smile wavered. Then he quickly recovered and nodded his head yes. "Understood," he said. "There'll be no problem. That's a promise."

"I'm a teacher. I know how people say 'Those who can, do. Those who can't, teach.' You're well off, and I'm not. No comments about teachers."

43

Bill felt teaching was his life's calling. He worked hard at it, making sure his students knew about the past, where we came from so they had some idea about the future and where we're going. Though he'd only been teaching at Conshe Mountain High for the past year, he hoped to coach eventually, too. He knew his work was important.

"Your profession is noble, and your business. The war cut short the ending years of my college days, but I have a high opinion of teachers and professors."

"I know you know about Jimmy Stevens, for everybody else seems to, how I pulled him around by his hair and the trouble that caused me. Now his uncle, who's chairman of the school board, will be on my case once school gets started. I anticipate that, at least. No comments about that, either, right?"

"None."

"And, please, no comments about my divorce."

Because Nell asked if he was married or not, Bill told her he was divorced. "My wife thought I have no ambition," he said. "She was right."

He should have picked up on something amiss when none but the most expensive engagement ring would do for her. He hadn't. Mary was gorgeous, the perfect girlfriend and fiancée. But it was almost as if she wanted pay-back for being what she was. Far from wanting to wrap her life around his, or even to share her life with his interests, she wanted him to dedicate himself and his whole career to bettering her financial condition. It would be nice, according to her, if he would leave the classroom, if he would take administrative positions, rising up the administrative ladder perhaps to the very top in the county where the pay was so much better.

He could think of nothing worse. When she saw what she

wanted wasn't going to be happening, she had walked out.

How he could have fooled himself so completely soured him on women and marriage. It made him miserable about himself, worst of all. When Nell suggested he could start dating again, he told her it was too soon, that he was a newcomer to a new place, and not interested.

"I'll say not a word," Sted promised.

"And as for Jessica Morgan, please, nothing about her. I don't care what she says, what anybody says. I'm not dating that woman. I'm no fan of hers. So nothing about her, either, agreed?"

"Bill, I don't even know who she is."

"She teaches English. God help me, in the classroom next to mine. What it is about English teachers, I don't know. I've never met a normal one. She's some kind of party girl. Makeup, lots of that. Expensive clothes, way too short and way too tight. She flirts openly with her male students, with me, and with Frank Wilkes… God, she's all over him. When I see a member of the faculty coming on to students, it angers me. I don't care if it's a male teacher or a female, I have to fight against telling them openly that's not what we're there for. I blame Wilkes for that, because I heard he's the one hired her. Any complaints about how she dresses or how she acts just get ignored. That's what I hear, anyway. There're rumors about her and me, but they're not true. I'm not the smartest man in the world, but even I know enough not to get involved with someone like her. The rumors irritate me."

"Quite a speech. I'll never mention her. Anything else?"

"No, that's the lot."

"And a hefty lot it is, but all reasonable. Good to know, so no mistakes are made. All perfectly acceptable." Sted grinned, rising from the table.

"End of the week, let's start then, Saturday. We'll start around nine or ten. Sound all right? Meantime, why don't you come to the cottage tomorrow morning, around ten, and we'll have lunch together, you, me, and Dalt, and we can show you around so you see what it would be like with those books."

Nell was smiling as Sted rose to leave, as if to say, *Told you so*.

"Meantime," Sted added, on his way out, "I hope you won't mind keeping that old history book someplace safe where we won't be moving it around over there till we can get somebody to look at it. I'll meet you at the dock, if the weather is good, tomorrow."

At quarter to ten the next day, when Bill docked Nell's little boat, Sted met him before he reached the porch steps.

"Come see the garden first," he said, "and then we'll go in, and Dalt will show you around inside while I fix some sandwiches." He led the way past tall mountain laurel bushes to an impressive gate. It was open, and a painted board, tied to its metal work, was easily readable, its black letters against a white background.

It read:

Then the conqueror sent them a message:

I could have taken you any time if I had wanted to.

The Spartans sent it back to him.

They had circled the word *if*.

"This is my *if* gate," Sted said. "That's such a powerful word. For the past, there's 'if only' such and such a thing hadn't happened, how much better life would be. And there's 'only if' we do such and such a thing can we be successful in the future. That, too. *If* is part of what's gone and what's yet to be." Sted was looking up at the statue, which was looming over the gate. It was positioned on a thick pedestal about four feet tall, making it dominant over most things around it. Its wings were posed as if in flight, its robes flowing, its face expectant.

"Are you a student of history, Sted?" Bill asked.

Sted turned and smiled. "Only my own," he replied.

It was Dalt who showed him around the cottage, and when Bill saw what a great number of books were involved, he became interested. He was amazed at how many there were. "All these books spread around everywhere else—did they come out of the library?" he asked.

"Not all," Dalt answered. "Books have always been everywhere here, not just the library. I've had plenty of reading days when I've been so alone, just me and a ton of books, rain day or snow day."

On a shelf at the top of the stairway, Bill noticed some leather-bound books. The title of one caught his eye: *Benedictus de Spinoza*. He slipped the book out to inspect it.

"My God," he said to Dalt, "here's an incredibly old book about the prince of philosophers."

Dalt was impressed by the softness of Bill's tone of voice, almost a whisper.

"I don't know who you're talking about. I'm such an uneducated man, and even Sted didn't get to finish college completely before the war, so who do you mean?"

Bill put the book back in its place gently. "The gentle Jew Spinoza. He led a difficult life. He believed happiness came through reason, not superstition, understanding we are all a part of nature, not masters of it."

"If you mean appreciating beauty, I had a lesson on that."

"Dalt, I noticed in Sted's bedroom there's even a book seems to be in Latin on parchment. God knows where that came from. Probably stolen from some monastery. Have any arrangements been made for an expert to come?"

"Lela is supposed to contact some antique dealers who may know somebody. There's nobody yet, but the work has to get done first, anyway."

"Somebody was a serious collector of books. Would that be you or Sted?"

"The only person I can think of was Sted's father. He got around more than anybody else here."

"I've seen her shop, Lela. She's an attractive person. You noticed her?"

Dalt blushed. "I'm still too embarrassed about my doomed marriage—"

"I'm just coming away from divorce myself," Bill admitted to him. "Not even allowing myself, either, to think …" They smiled at each other as if they were brothers in the same suffering club. Then Sted called them from below. He had iced tea and sandwiches, and they ate on the lovely wide porch.

When Bill began working every day except weekends at the cottage, he wasn't sure which he liked more, the open breeziness of every room in the place and the architectural attention to details that pleased the eye or the variety and age of the books he was handling. At the beginning of his working for Sted and Dalt, Bill reflected on what Ricky had said, "He had it in his mind you reminded him of the son he never got to see."

"Is he all right mentally?" Bill had asked. "Is that what we're talking about here?"

"Sted wouldn't hurt a fly," Ricky had assured Bill. "He'll probably enjoy having people around, you and Lela, not just him and Dalt, you know."

"Think so?"

"Yeah."

Nonetheless, at first Bill was a little leery, but Sted worked earnestly on the books, just as Bill and Dalt and Lela did. Bill relaxed. It was good summer money, and he could start each day fishing awhile, if he wanted to. Nobody objected to it, for these three unmarried men were believers in fishing. Ricky was on the porch many mornings, begging the others to come fish or going around the lake on his own. It was all lenient and comfortable.

Bill began to like Sted, to respect him. Anyone who had a collection of this size and scope—such fine old books—deserved respect.

Besides, Sted wasn't sticking around in his spare time trying to be pals with Bill. He began taking some long walks in the woods. So Ricky was right, Bill decided. Sted wouldn't hurt a fly.

He might have been less comfortable if he knew how pleased Sted was that Bill was so talkative, and that he was such a protected presence in the cottage, working away day after day. For that was important, that protection, to Sted.

Only Nell sensed an important thing about Sted as he entered her house. She felt right away that Sted wanted a good look at Bill Accardi even more than he wanted Bill to have a look at that book. And if that was what Sted wanted, he was certainly successful.

6

Ruben, Ruben, I've been thinking
What a fine world this would be
If the men could all be taken
Far beyond the northern sea.

A few days after Sted was with Nell and Bill at her house, Dalt entered Lela Sterling's little antique shop. Dalt hadn't talked to her since long ago when she came to the cottage to explain finances to him. He remembered that meeting very well, even though that was in the 1950s. Sted must have had lawyers and bankers putting pressure on him to take care of things then, and thank God for Lela. She was young but very helpful. He was attracted to her even then, but he felt inferior, listening to her as she took the role of teacher, and he sat as a student would sit. He was stingingly embarrassed about his farce of a failed marriage back then, too.

Women, Dalt felt, give off signals even they themselves might not understand, if they wanted to know a man better. Then, when she was so much younger, she gave no signals to him, and now he wondered if that would still be the case. His admiration of her was a definite thing.

If women were sailing vessels, Dalt had skippered quite a few. The loneliness he sometimes felt at the cottage drove him to answer many a flirty call given to him. It would be nice, he sometimes admitted to himself, if there were no signals being sent.

Lela was, of course, older now, he noticed as she greeted him, but she was still attractive. Her short, curly red hair framed an interesting face, and she had green eyes, kissable lips, and an upturned nose. In fact, she had such an impact on Dalt, he wondered if he could do what Sted wanted. It seemed like a petty mission. Suddenly, he felt his confidence slip away, and he didn't want Lela to see him on such an errand, but it was too late now.

Sted heard that Frank Wilkes had his eye on a real Persian rug Lela had in her shop. That meant Sted suddenly wanted it himself. Dalt guessed Sted wanted to get the rug because that would irritate Wilkes. The instructions were to pay whatever was necessary to get that rug.

God knows Lela could use some extra money to run her shop. Conshe Mountain was far away from the usual tourist paths. That was great for keeping the lake from being overfished, but bad for those who had quilts and antiques and apple butter to sell. More people came to sell an heirloom through her shop than came to buy one. She was a capable lawyer and financial whiz, though, and made a decent living giving legal and financial advice. Her little shop wasn't her only income. She needed no man to pay her bills. She was educated and independent. Her intelligence and education intimidated Dalt.

In a small town like Conshe, word gets around. Dalt heard that a fellow named Jack loved her and wanted Lela to move to Pittsburgh with him, but it hadn't worked out. That was because of a dog. Some people said the man wanted no dog, and it was him or the dog, and she chose the dog. Others said she was willing to leave the dog behind, but she couldn't find anybody who would take the dog because it was so mean. Either way, a fourteen-pound dog kept her where she was. What made Lela so compassionate about the dog, people said, was that his horrible behavior came from the best of dog intentions: he was so devoted to her and his new-found home (he was a rescued dog) he viewed everybody as an enemy. Grudgingly, Dalt admitted to himself it was refreshing to find someone who wouldn't even double-cross a dog, not even a mean one.

He'd been warned about its bite. Tim said it didn't really break through the skin, but it was sneaky and would attack your leg or your foot or ankle, leaving red pinch marks. "That dog belongs in Australia or someplace like that," Tim proclaimed, "herding sheep or something."

The dog, looking much like some stuffed white toy, was lying on a red love seat, eyeing Dalt as he entered the shop. Its head was up, and its little dark button eyes were focused on the man. Its apple-shaped head was covered with the softest spiked hair, and its ears were hanging covered with ringlets. On each side of its nose there were bushy side chops, and there was a fountain of a longer-haired tail, like an explosion of silken strands hanging over its hips.

Women, seeing this dog, knowing nothing of it, cried out, "Oh, such a cute dog!"

Not so, said all those who had been attacked by it, including the mailman and Jack-who-escaped-to-Pittsburgh.

The little dog's name was Ruben. That was a name Dalt had never heard before applied to a dog, and he said to himself it probably meant "ankle taster." He'd been told if he stayed very still he'd be safe. Like being near elephants or lions, he decided. Close by the entrance to the shop, he found a seat near a pile of quilted coverlets, and there he intended to stay.

Lela remembered him and reminded him of some conversation he couldn't recall in a grocery store or some such place. Unwisely, he asked her about the dog.

"Did you name him that?" he asked. "Had him long? He's so… cute."

"No, he came with the name, and I didn't want to confuse him. He's been my good friend since Mom's death." The dog yawned and stretched its short forelegs. "Oh, I think he likes you," she said.

The conversation eventually came around to the Persian rug. Dalt could see it, as a matter of fact, from where he sat. It was rolled up, propped in a corner with other less beautiful rugs. Yes, Lela said, it was truly a Persian rug and very expensive, and she was so lucky to get it. She was at an estate sale, and there were no other antique dealers there that day, so she was able to afford it.

Unfortunately, Lela had a conscience. That rug was promised to Frank Wilkes.

Dalt switched from friendly conversation to common sense. "I'm sure Sted wants this rug because Frank Wilkes does. But that doesn't matter. If Mr. Wilkes hasn't put any money down on the rug, if he hasn't actually paid you anything toward it, then you're not obligated to him in any way." Her eyes widened and Dalt felt more confident.

"I don't know how much Mr. Wilkes has offered you, but I have a thousand dollars from Sted with me right now. And I can add another thousand from my own pocket for… hmm… this pile of coverlets right here, all four of them. How's that? Remember how expensive dogs can be. There's grooming, and shots, and food. The money goes fast!"

She hesitated, and Dalt knew she would agree. She walked to the rugs, where they were standing, rolled up, in the corner. He got a good view, Dalt did, of flowing leg lines coming away from

53

her trim stern. Yes, he was looking at her as if she were as pretty a little sailing vessel as could be, and then, forgetting the warnings he'd been given, he stood up to go help her get that rug out from the pile of other rugs. That was a big mistake. The little dog silently slid off the love seat and bit him on his left ankle.

Without even thinking about it, Dalt's foot shot out and connected with the little white fluffy head before Ruben could get away. It must have made a sharp impression because the dog yelped.

"Oh, I stepped on his tail," Dalt lied. She scooped up the dog, comforting it.

"Poor Ruben," she sing-songed. The dog was pretending to be hurt, pretending to be loving, licking her hand, rolling his eyes at Dalt. She sat on the red love seat, petting him. The dog beside her was glaring at Dalt, a possessive paw on her leg.

What does one do, Dalt wondered, when an attractive woman was sitting there, looking so attentive, her face receptive and listening, but giving no signals? There was no licking of the lips, no eye-batting, no fluttering of lashes, no silken hand caressing its own cheek, no casual flipping of stray hair.

Best, then, to go ahead and talk about the other thing she might find interesting. He needed to talk about the books. She might want to consider spending some time helping with the books project, for it would pay very well. He explained how it would be necessary to get the books in piles, in categories, and when done, then perhaps each person could keep one collectible book for one's own, as an item of interest or an investment. And could she help find an expert to examine and evaluate the books, also? He tried to be friendly and convincing because he wanted to work alongside her.

There was one bargaining point. The little white dog had to

come with her when she came to the cottage. Well, that was what leashes were for, he reasoned.

Done!

Heaven forbid the nasty little beast should be lonely.

Dalt didn't want to be piling books way into November, and the more helpers, the better; especially if the helper were someone pleasant and attractive.

At the front of her shop, there was a large window, one that reached from the ceiling to the floor. The tiny white head of Ruben the dog was peering out at the bottom of that window as the rug and the quilts were put into Dalt's car. Once the door to the shop was closed and Lela was walking away into the interior, Dalt fixed the dog with a malevolent stare. With both hands, he made a twisting motion as if cranking little Ruben's head off. The dog's ears lifted, its eyes rolled, and it fled.

Told the little dog would be part of the deal if Lela came to work on the books, Sted shrugged. How much trouble could one small dog be? Dalt laughed to himself, wondering if they should buy some sheep the dog could herd. Then he took the expensive rug and put it into the hay room, still rolled up. That was where Sted wanted it to be, though that seemed strange. Dalt wouldn't have put such a rug there, but it wasn't his call. Sted was paying the bills, just as he paid for the rug. Sted probably didn't care about the rug at all, just as he didn't care, really, about most things.

It was Nell and Tim and he, really, who kept the cottage together. Nell kept Dalt informed when things weren't right, and it was up to him to get those things fixed or fix them himself. A home so graciously old doesn't stay that way as it gets older and older. That takes money and work. That was why the downstairs bathroom was remodeled, but the bathrooms upstairs still had the old claw-footed bathtubs in them. That was why all the electrical circuits had to be brought up to code, and why there was a new furnace. Two years ago, a new roof went on the cottage, and that bill was so high, even Sted stomped around for days over it.

Dalt had been living in the house since before the ninth grade, and he'd grown to love it, but after everyone was gone and he was left alone in it, he'd come to appreciate companionship. Dalt sometimes hungered for simple friendship, even as he brought into the cottage female after female.

It was in the name of friendship he began collecting the things that were found in the dining room. Those were things such as crayons, toys, and nursery books. He'd thought about that crayoned drawing Nell found. He looked, and there weren't any crayons in the house. Those crayons, he felt sure, came out of Sted's pockets.

Dalt took Nell into his confidence. "Sted's had bad dreams before," Dalt told her, "after the war. After a while, those stopped. Maybe this is like that."

Nell's hand sometimes trembled as she showed him some toy she'd found. Dalt tried explaining Sted was probably groggy when he woke from a dream, and when he went into the dining room, maybe he deluded himself into thinking there had been a child there. Nell seemed to accept that.

Sometimes, in the morning, when Sted was falling asleep as he sat in a rocker on the porch, Dalt figured he'd had a bad time with dreams again.

Then Dalt would cast his mind back to when Sted stopped caring, back to Faye's death and the awful argument that followed. Sted had left for college without saying goodbye to anyone. And then, when the war began, he left again, saying nothing.

Dalt was hurt when he never heard from Sted during those war years.

Even worse, Dalt witnessed the suffering of two parents who never heard from Sted and never saw their son again.

7

Lincoln said that turtle's life was as dear to him as our lives are to us, and he thrashed the bully who smashed the turtle against a tree, crushing its shell and killing it.

Sted was huddled against a bank of flowering bushes, waiting in the moonlight. There were deeper shadows where he positioned himself, so he knew he wouldn't be spotted.

He imagined how Jimmy Stevens would approach. Probably he'd ride his bike on the county paved road, and then he'd leave it alongside in the weeds. He'd walk up the dirt service road. He'd pass fencing on both sides of that road meant for livestock once upon a time. Then the fencing on the right would stretch away in that direction and give way to what once were the stables, now the long garage. The car and the pick-up were in there, lost in all that space. There were four garage doors, all down and locked.

At the far end of, and within the dimly lit garage, was the stable tack room. Jimmy would be able to see into that room, where there was an enclosed toilet, shower, shelves and tables, but that door was locked, too.

He would cross the space where the big tiles marked a pathway to the back kitchen door, and he would reach what once was a barn but now was a smaller space they called the hay room, and that was also locked.

Another open space, and he would reach garden sheds, three

of them, one of which was a heated greenhouse. These, also, were locked.

So Jimmy would appear between the gardening sheds and the south side of the cottage. He would come around the corner where Sted couldn't help but see him.

Sted had everything he needed. Next to the dock, he'd placed about one hundred feet of cord, the sort used for clotheslines. On the dock were two tarps, one of which he could use. Alongside the dock, lying in a sort of path design, were heavy tiles left over from the kitchen pathway construction. Between two garden sheds, there was a hammock strung up where one landscaper liked to relax during his lunch break. And the two anchors were lying on the dock, also.

In his pocket was a folding, very sharp pen knife and the gun.

There was a full moon, and the sweep of the lawn, including the flower beds and the angel statue were speckled with light and shifting shadows fanned by a pleasant breeze. There was a faint smell of some jasmine or clematis blooming vine.

This was the second night he'd been watching, and he was sure Jimmy wouldn't be able to resist the temptation of going on the prowl on such a moonlit night.

He thought he heard noises from the gardening sheds, as if someone had tried a couple of doors and given them a little tug, not happy that he couldn't do what he'd been doing whenever he trespassed before. It was enough noise to make Sted alert. He clutched the gun.

On the second floor of the cottage, soft music was playing and could be heard through an open window. Dalt was aware Sted was on patrol again. He understood that if the youth showed up, Sted would put a couple of shots in the air to frighten him away. Dalt could be seen, partially dressed, moving around between his bathroom and his bedroom. He had no reason to believe he'd be needed outside.

Sted had added something as bait. Light from the dining room below Dalt's bedroom shone down on a lounge chair on the lawn below it. Lying there, on the lounge chair, as if carelessly left, forgotten, was a shoebox. Its lid was off, and one shoe of a pair of expensive athletic shoes was sticking up, as if someone had been trying on the shoes. If Jimmy came around the corner of the cottage, he couldn't help but see that shoebox.

There was movement at that spot Sted was watching. Jimmy appeared, wearing a hooded mid-calf light coat, the hood down. However, he was wearing a baseball cap, its brim shading his eyes. At first cautious, looking about, he finally walked out into the open. He looked up, seeing Dalt moving past the windows upstairs, hearing the music. Then he spotted the shoebox.

He sat down on the lounge chair and inspected the shoes. Sted had positioned that chair so Jimmy's back would be turned toward him. When he saw the youngster had taken off one of his shoes and was struggling to try on one of the athletic shoes, Sted moved out of the shadows, not too quickly, but quietly.

Jimmy was seated, turned away from Sted, and concentrating on something other than his safety. He was taken by surprise when Sted poked the gun barrel into his back.

Sted didn't want to shoot him in the back. That would be too obvious. So, as the boy turned, looking to see who was threatening him, Sted shot him in the side.

He screamed, and Sted forced him off the lounge down to the ground, putting his free hand over his mouth. "No one to help you here," he muttered. The second shot went into the side of Jimmy's head.

Dalt certainly heard that scream. When he came running

down the front porch steps, the boy was still kicking and making noises. By that time, Sted had knocked the lounge chair aside and pulled and twisted his shirt as if there had been a struggle.

Dalt was struck dumb for a minute. Then he cried out, "My God! What happened?" The dying boy continued to struggle for a while, making noises, trying to talk, to breathe, to live.

"He went for the gun!" Sted exclaimed. "I got too close! I had no choice. He actually got his hand on the gun!"

"We have to go get help!" Dalt said, desperately frightened.

"Help, hell! He can't be helped. Do you want me carted off to jail? We have to get rid of his body! And stop yelling so loud!"

"We've killed him," Dalt whispered several times as if he couldn't believe it.

Now he followed Sted's lead, trusting him as he always had throughout his life, not questioning anything, just as Sted thought he might. Sted used his pen knife to cut away the fastenings and brought down the hammock that was hanging between the sheds. He placed Jimmy's still body on the hammock, on the ground, and then pulled the body over to the dock, dragging the hammock over the grass. Once there, he placed some of the heavy path tiles into the hammock so that they accompanied the body. He rolled the hammock around the body and the tiles, and then he used his pen knife to cut lengths of the cording to tie the body into the hammock securely.

"I can't do this alone," he said to Dalt. "You'll have to help me."

He opened the smaller tarp there on the ground near the dock, and then he rolled the hammock-wrapped body into one side of the tarp. The two men worked together, breathing heavily. They laboriously moved the tarp around Jimmy, tucking in the top and then rolling, tucking in the bottom, spinning and turning

61

the body, tucking and turning, till they had no more tarp to use. More cording was used in several places to tie everything tightly and securely. Jimmy's wrappings made his body look as if it was a roast about to be put into an oven.

"I'm sorry, I'm sorry," Sted said several times. "I wish you weren't involved in this. But I'm so glad you're here to help. I'd do the same for you. You know that."

The little boat was in the water beside the dock. The hardest thing was to get that body into the boat without tipping it over. Then, Sted tied one anchor at the head of the body and the other one at the foot. Each man used an oar as a paddle would be used, standing or squatting, balancing over the body, getting it out into the deepest center of the lake. It was risky, for they could fall into the water with a great deal of noise if they lost their balance. Where they felt it was deepest, they managed to get the body out of the boat into the water, which caused a lot of splashing. At first, the body refused to sink until it was turned in such a way the anchors dragged it down.

Dalt kept thinking there would be a spotlight or flashlight suddenly shining on them from Nell's house, but no lights went on over there. Sted sat in the boat in a more conventional way, rowing back to his own dock, and Dalt was leaning over the water, using his hands to help propel the boat back to their property.

Dalt made it to the few lawn chairs on the lawn between the dock and the cottage. He fell into one of them, joined a moment later by Sted dropping into the second chair. They were both exhausted, and there they rested for a minute or two, not talking at all.

Finally, they struggled up the front porch steps and made it, at last, into the kitchen, where both felt safe. Dalt made coffee with trembling hands.

"I'm not going to sleep till dawn and I see that body isn't floating on the surface," he declared. "If that body surfaces and anyone sees it, we're screwed."

"I had to shoot him! I never intended for this to happen! It could have been me dead! I just got lucky."

Dalt believed him. But he couldn't help but express his personal anguish. "My God, Sted, we've cut off a young life before he really had a chance to live it. And what if those shots were heard?"

"Bullshit! He did that to himself. I refuse to let us take the blame. He could see we knew he was around when he saw everything was locked up, but he came on anyway. Should have been a better person. And we don't admit to hearing any shots."

"But what if later on he changed—"

"If! He was what he was, Dalt, and later on would probably be more of the same. It's done, and we have to live with it."

"Police may come—"

"They certainly will. You can count on this one thing—that boy never left a note on his kitchen table saying he was coming over here to pick on us. When the police come, let me handle it."

"Gladly."

They were awake at dawn. The body was still below. Even so, Dalt was afraid fishermen would snag their lines on the wrappings at the bottom of the lake.

Sted reassured him. "A fisherman will cut his line, be willing to lose some equipment, for he'll tell right away it isn't getting loose whatever it is, and it isn't coming up, either." Dalt believed him because there was nothing else to hope for.

Later, Sted gathered in the shoes, making sure there was no blood on them or on the shoebox. He used a scoop to dig up soil and grass where the boy bled and died. He dumped that in the lake. In a day or so, he'd put some fresh dirt where that spot was. At the edge of the dock, he found Jimmy's baseball cap. He later stuck that in a hole alongside and slightly under the hay room. He covered it with soil and tamped it down.

The day after Jimmy's death, during the day, Sted walked down to the county road. He found the bike. He walked it some distance away from the service road, facing the opposite direction and on the opposite side of the road, as if Jimmy had been going toward town. Sted wiped the handlebars, all he'd touched, and tossed it off the road, so that it would be hard, but not impossible, to find.

The morning after the boy's death, Nell's mother complained about noise on the lake during the night. She said she didn't know what Sted was thinking of, going swimming at night. No one paid much attention to her. No one mentioned hearing any shots.

The next time Nell and Tim came to work, Tim noticed at once things were not quite as they should be in the hay room, but he was so pleased with the new athletic shoes Sted got for him he forgot all about that. The shoes fit him.

The two men were reacting differently to the death of the bully. Sted was cheerful and happy. Dalt, not so. He kept imagining how it must feel to go check on your child and discover his bed is not slept in, and he's missing. Dalt also wondered if he would ever be able to fish in the lake again without fear that his line would get caught on something, and now he began having bad dreams about it.

Of course, eventually the police got around to questioning them. Police Chief Don Axel himself came to call. He'd heard Jimmy had boasted about being a trespasser here at the cottage. Yes, Sted agreed; they'd heard about that, too. They'd started locking everything up at night and had no problem after that. No sign of anything being disturbed or stolen.

Later, when it was discovered that Jimmy was not promoted into ninth grade, everyone supposed he was a runaway. His bike wasn't noticed, not for years.

Also, later, Sted bought two more anchors. He stopped and mentioned to the police chief that he had to amend his report that nothing was stolen. But he didn't think Jimmy had actually bothered to cart off those two heavy anchors. He probably just tossed them somewhere in the lake. The word was that Jimmy did mean things sometimes. Perhaps that was one of those things.

Tim had inherited a noticing eye from his mother, and he saw right away those two anchors were different from the way the previous two anchors had looked. And he commented on the heavy paving tiles that were leftovers from the completion of the kitchen pathway; those were lying around in front of the dock like some sort of crazy sidewalk. And, of course, there was all that clothesline.

He voiced those thoughts to Dalt, and now Dalt began picking mentally on some things that were bothersome. How was it, indeed, those pathway tiles were there in such a convenient spot, just asking to be used? For that matter, where did all that cord come from that was used to tie everything up so tightly?

When he asked, he couldn't help but notice Sted was irritated at those questions.

He didn't want to waste those tiles, Sted explained. He thought they could be used to make a path from the dock to the porch, but as soon as he started putting them down, even though he hadn't dragged all of them to the dock, he could see he didn't have enough tiles to get the job done, so he stopped. He'd tied some of them together at a time with cord to get them out there, and intended to use cord to drag them back. But once he tried to move those heavy tiles again, he got discouraged, and he just left the cord and the tiles out there at the dock.

Dalt didn't notice a hammock was gone.

It was the look Sted shot at Dalt that troubled him. That look sort of said, "Got that, have you now?" without words.

He'd never known Sted to care enough about the cottage to put forth that much effort.

It could be about something else, then. Dalt remembered when they first came to live at the cottage, everybody had to deal with an astonishing number of mice. The mice had lived there for a long time without people around, apparently. At first, he and Sted had sympathy for any tiny mouse they'd catch in a trap, figuring the little creature loved life, same as they did.

But there were so many mice, after a while they got so they cared less and less about their deaths. They began trapping them with very little feeling for them.

My, how cheerful Sted was the day after Jimmy Stevens's death.

Could a person get so he felt that way about people, too, as if they were mice?

8

How's he usin' all this stuff?

Two days later, the sun promised a pleasant morning, but it soon became overcast and humid. Nell and Tim arrived for work, as usual, and Nell almost immediately found a toy in the dining room.

"I don't think Sted's bad dreams are letting up any," she commented to Dalt as she handed it to him. "Maybe it's even worse, just changed some. The things now are for an older child. So it isn't stopping. It's just changing."

Dalt dealt with what she said as being true. "I can see I'm going to have to talk about this with him," he said sadly. "He probably doesn't know we're aware of what's happening with him."

Nell didn't seem assured. She shook her head as she went into the kitchen.

Dalt's stomach began churning.

Ricky didn't help. Dalt always made time to fish with Ricky, but since the Stevens boy's death, the last thing Dalt wanted was to fish in that lake. He was beginning to have bad dreams of his own, awful visions of bubbles, things rising up, coming to the top. Now Ricky hove into view, coming in from the porch, persistently asking when Dalt was going to take time to fish this morning before the fish lost interest. Even when Dalt said he wasn't feeling well (and that was becoming true), Ricky was openly skeptical. "Who you foolin'?" he quipped. "You're *never* sick."

Tim was the worst. He was protesting, but he wasn't sure against what. "Something's wrong around here," he said. "Your boat doesn't need caulking at all. You and Sted never use it in the middle of the lake, anyway. It just sits there at the dock for ages. We're always fishing with waders in the shallows."

Tim included himself as one of the fishermen, for he joined them whenever he could. He had also become a regular fishing partner of Bill's.

He regarded the dock with a prejudiced eye. "There were two tarps here, and now there's one, and those anchors aren't the same. And what's with these kitchen path tiles layin' around there? What are *they* doin' way up there? And what's with all this *clothesline* doin' there? "

Told that perhaps Sted was working on something in the area, he answered that with, "Oh? What's he *doin'* with all this stuff, then?"

After he put the clothesline cord away in the hay room, he came back to Dalt again. "There's *more* stuff there in the hay room," he said, eyes widened. "More tarps, and lots more cord, and there's some rope, too."

Dalt felt his legs start quivering as Tim went on and on.

"Well, let's just say it's his business now, isn't it? Not for us to say what Sted's up to all the time, now is it?" He fled to the kitchen for coffee, always his safe haven. There he met Bill, emerging up the stairs from the storage area under the kitchen where books had been stored, and where Bill was now making separate piles of them. He was carrying some into the common room.

"Look!" he exclaimed. "This is what turned up!" He was

carrying books in a canvas tote. "This is a series of books on Poe. The complete works of Poe! Some are missing, but still, this is great!" For a moment, Dalt joined in with his excitement.

But it was only a temporary excitement. Dalt hadn't even finished his cup of coffee before here came Tim again.

"You'd better come look at this," he said. He wasted no words, just led Dalt out into the garden to the foot of the angel statue.

"He's had me dig this trench for roses," he muttered. "Now when I come here today, look what's in it."

"What's in it" turned out to be that expensive Persian rug. It had been dumped into the trench. Clearly, it was tamped down so that it would fit in the trench under all the dirt that would be dumped in on top of it. For a minute, Dalt sipped his coffee. Then he sighed and said to the waiting Tim, "Would you go find Sted and ask him to come out here? He might be upstairs, working on books in the bedrooms."

In time, Sted and Tim arrived, Sted frowning.

"You paid good money for this rug," Dalt complained. "And this is where the rug ends up?"

Tim was intently listening.

"Well, roses love water. I thought it would help hold water in there for the roses."

"A two thousand-dollar rug for a water holder?"

"Then, dammit, you two take it out of there and put it back in the hay room! Maybe I'll listen to Wilkes. He called me, all mad about my buying that rug, and I threw it in there because he made me mad. I'll just probably let Wilkes have it. So put it back! All right?"

Tim just couldn't remain quiet. "This is a bad place for a row of roses, anyway! It's right across the middle of her!"

"Her?"

"Faye! You told me she's under here, out in this direction with her feet out here." Tim tapped on the grass where he stood with his foot. "Why put roses right across the middle of where she is, anyway? And why's all that stuff in the hay room, anyway?"

"Oh, for Christ's sake. All right, all right, we won't put roses there. Just take the rug out, and then fill the bed in with dirt again! Fill the damn thing in! Forget it!" Sted turned away and marched back to the cottage and the books upstairs.

"Why's he doin' all this stuff, anyway?" Tim asked again, forlornly.

Back in the cottage, as Dalt crossed the common room, Lela looked out from the dining room, where some of the books were piled. She was finishing up in there. The little dog Ruben was under the dining table. He wasn't so sure of himself in a new place and was keeping quiet, sticking close to Lela.

She read the sour expression on Dalt's face. "Are you upset about something?" she asked him. "Are you all right?"

He decided to tell her.

"That rug I got from you that Sted wanted? He put it into a trench he had Tim dig to plant roses in. Stupid. It's not in there now, though. It's been taken out, saved."

She was distressed.

"Money doesn't matter to him, not much, anyway. But that rug deserved better treatment than that," Dalt complained.

She sat down at the table where books were scattered, some with paper tags sticking out of them. The little dog was at her feet. He and Dalt eyed each other. Dalt sat down, making sure he had his feet pulled in close to the chair.

"Ruben's been very good," she said.

"I have to tell you something else," Dalt said impulsively. It had to be told. He couldn't go on without saying it, regardless of the consequences.

"I didn't step on your dog's tail. He bit me, and I kicked him. And I'm not sorry one bit. I liked it when I thought you had a good opinion of me, but Lela, he's a horrible dog. Right now, he's snuggled up against your foot, the little bastard, being quiet because he remembers I kicked him. He doesn't like me, like you said in your shop. He doesn't like anybody in this world except you, and that's the truth. He's probably planning something. That's why he's quiet."

Ah, confession felt good.

She rose from her seat. "Stand up, please," she said.

"What?"

"Please just stand up. You'll see. Please."

Dalt stood warily. At attention. Sort of. Almost.

"I love hugs." She came closer. "I'm going to hug you, and maybe you'll hug me back." She put herself in the circle of his arms, her hair brushing against his chin, smelling of some flowery shampoo or cologne. "You're a good person, except for kicking Ruben. Sted and his family are lucky to have you."

He wanted to kiss her hair. She was hugging him, her arms around him tight. Her head was buried in his chest; she was talking to his torso. He wanted to hug her. Something, perhaps his age, the feeling he would be rejected, stopped him from putting his arms tightly around her and hugging her back.

"God help me. What are you starting here?" he whispered, mostly to himself.

Then she pulled away, smiling. She announced they must have a pot of tea, sharing a cup of tea together. "Please sit down and wait a bit," she said. "Promise me you won't go off."

When she returned, he was still there, still seated and looking a little confused. Ruben was sitting on the floor, regarding Dalt with his head cocked to one side, making no move to bite him or to bark.

There are times when a bad day is so bad you give in to it.

When Tim had asked, "What's he doing with all this stuff?" Dalt knew he had no answer. When he, Dalt, asked himself if Sted was being honest about the Stevens boy's death, he had no answer for that, either.

When he looked at himself in the mirror, as he had been doing lately, he asked himself if his life had any meaning at all. He was unmarried, had no children, and most of his life so far centered around this family, this cottage. What happened to him when the last of that family crumbled away? Was there anything else he could do? He had no answer for that, either.

So a cup of tea might be just the thing. It seemed all right to relax with her.

"All right if we move into the kitchen, then? To my favorite chair, my rocker in there. Just bring the tea with us." Somehow, he needed to signal his age. He settled into the chair. "Old man's chair. You know how it is with us old men."

Didn't work. She laughed. "I'm fifty-four, not so young myself. I know you're older than me, but you have many years to go, Dalt."

She sipped her tea, then added, "It's a dangerous world, no matter what our ages are. We can't go around cringing, you know. You're a handsome man, and you still have love to give, Dalt."

He suddenly remembered there were crackers in the cabinet. "In the refrig, I think there's some cheese," he said. "You want to check on that, and I'll get the crackers?"

The tea was good, and his mood lightened. She had that

magical effect on him. He mentioned his lack of a higher education, but that didn't faze her, either.

"Sometimes we don't get much of a say about what happens to us in this life," she said. "The war sucked Sted in. He had no say about that. The cottage sucked you in, and you didn't get to choose that, either, now, did you? It takes a heroic effort to have control, don't you think, over what happens to us? I think life uses us."

He wanted to reach over and touch her, and he wished he had hugged her back.

"Well, it's back to work," she said finally.

When he went upstairs to work on the books, he was in a much better mood because of her. He felt strongly about her, but he kept putting off any hugs coming from him. Now he was tired of being such a coward. That included what he'd promised himself and Nell that he would do about Sted.

He put it off until nightfall, until there was this humid, hot night when nobody was sleepy, anyway. Nell and Tim had gone back home across the lake. Now he tried to talk to Sted.

"Nell and I find items in the dining room. And that causes us some concern," he began.

Sted was resentful; that was clear. Dalt pressed on, anyway. "Maybe when you wake up from dreams, Sted, you're not fully awake, even when you're walking around. And when you think a child is there in the dining room, there really isn't one."

"No, he's real."

"He can't be, Sted. That's not possible."

"It's true, though. He tells me everything I need to get things done. All I have to do. He's real."

"What? He tells you… what? What does he say to you?"

"That's none of your business."

Dalt didn't tell Sted that sometimes now he was awake himself due to horrible dreams. That he could hear those pocket doors when they were pulled back into the wall, when they hit the barrier there within the walls that stopped them. Always there was that bumping sound.

Then he wondered if Sted was there, talking and listening in the dining room.

Talking and listening to what? he wondered.

9

Into the Woods, a Heart of Stone

Bill Accardi was both excited and puzzled. In the attic, he went exploring and found yet another trove of books. They were against a far wall, covered with old quilts. Lela, Bill thought, might like the quilts, even though they looked yellowed and rotten to him.

He scouted up Sted as soon as he'd taken a good look. "Sted! There's all kinds of British naval books! Some on Nelson, and one book I saw was letters from Nelson to his lover, Lady Hamilton! And I saw at least one more Poe book!"

Sted groaned. Yet he followed Bill. What he saw meant more work, and those books had to be taken down from a hot attic. The window at that end of the attic wouldn't open. The heat was awful.

"I say this bunch has to be moved at night, maybe."

"The longer they stay here, the worse it is for them."

"They've been here this long, longer won't matter. Maybe we need to take a break anyway. It's a mess."

"No, it's a treasure!" Bill exclaimed. "Dalt said he thinks it's your father who collected all these. He must have had some connection to the British navy. You must be proud of having such a dad!"

He was puzzled by the look Sted shot his way. It was almost threatening. Bill felt hairs on his neck rise. He suddenly felt unsafe and changed the subject quickly. "I notice you have some books on your bedroom window sill. So what do you want us to do with them?"

"I'm keeping them," Sted replied as they left the attic. "I never realized there were so many. Let's do this sensibly. We'll get these down at night or when it rains. And then we'll put them into their categories when we get them downstairs. What I'd really like to do is go fishing before we start in on more of them."

When Bill saw Dalt later, as soon as he saw they were alone, he asked Dalt about that look he got from Sted. "I could almost see some hate in that look I got. Didn't he get along with his father?"

Dalt could imagine that look. "Sted's father never showed much emotion," he explained. "Sted never got much affection from his mother and father. But that doesn't mean they didn't love him." In his mind, he saw Helen's face brightening every time they heard some bit of news about Sted during the war years.

"There were only a couple of times I ever saw his father give way to his emotions," Dalt continued, and he remembered Reginald Robbins with tears running down his face at Helen's funeral. Earlier, at that horrible holiday argument following Faye's death, as Dalt kept Sted away from his aunt, he remembered hearing Reginald's voice shouting at his sister-in-law, "Shut up, Eva! For God's sake, shut up!"

"There's some quilts up in the attic," Bill remarked as he digested that family news. "I bet Lela would like to see those."

Dalt seemed to be withdrawing from unpleasant thoughts. He smiled. "I'll tell her."

"You like her, don't you? You're attracted to her. Why don't you tell her?"

Dalt's cheekbones reddened. "Well, yes. But you have

degrees, not me. Nothing beyond high school. And I'm old. And I have a bit of a reputation about women."

"From what Nell tells me, you had a job, all right, taking care of things here, tending to those people who owned this place. And as for the women, I bet they were tracking you, Dalt. Nell says you're one of the good guys. For a minute, I felt peculiar with Sted. I think you're… different from him. In a better way. He doesn't have to know I feel that way."

They went to the porch to eat lunch out where it was cool. Ricky was visiting, already there, and Ruben was by the door. "Me and your dog are gettin' tired of waitin' for lunch," Ricky loudly complained.

"He's not my dog."

Nonetheless, the dog settled near Dalt's chair as they sat down, till Lela called him from inside the house. Bill smiled to himself, for he saw Ruben pause at the door, looking back at Dalt before he went away.

Sted was tired. He'd been tired all afternoon, and as night fell, he was happy to go to bed right after his supper. He thought he'd sleep well. He didn't. He woke in the middle of the night, shaking with anger. He dreamt Frank Wilkes was in pursuit of Sted's son, a young man looking like Bill Accardi, pursuing the boy all over a building that looked like a school or offices. There were lots of rooms and closets. Poor Bill kept trying to hide, and Wilkes kept finding him. Sted woke when Wilkes had Bill trapped in a store room of some sort.

When Sted woke, he was so angry he threw off his covers, left his bedroom and stomped into the adjoining sunroom, and from there into the kitchen. At first, he sat in the rocker by the windows, but he couldn't settle down. He hurried to the dining room. The pocket doors were closed. He opened them.

77

A voice, sounding perhaps like a youth's, said, "Hi, Dad."
He closed the doors behind himself.

Frank Wilkes had a profitable business supplying restaurants and
motels in the area with clean linens. It pretty much ran itself, so
he had plenty of time to be chairman of the school board and be
a solid family man. His skinny wife, his divorced sister and her
son enjoyed his generosity. He doted on his nephew, Jimmy, and
he had close chummy contact with school administrators and
teachers. Frank expected, and often got, adulation from faculty.
If you acknowledged his importance and showed gratitude for
your job, he could be your friend. If you didn't, you could expect
trouble.

Not that Frank would be unfaithful to his wife. He would
never go that far. She was a woman as small and skinny as he
was fat, and he was protective of her. But there were two female
teachers who had suffered throughout the past school year
because, so far as he knew, neither of them had ever said one
good word about him. The first one, a beginning teacher, was told
by him she might not be hired for the coming year, because there
had been so many complaints about her competence. He would
speak up for her, he said, if she wanted him to, provided he came
to observe her classes and offer ways to improve. The second
woman, attractive and middle-aged, was warned by Frank that a
parent was upset by her son's complaints that she was too
familiar with him.

None of the things Frank told the women were true. His
moral standards were slack, to say the least. He encouraged a few
administrators he knew well to give good references for the
faculty members they wanted to get rid of and to give lousy
references for faculty members they wanted to keep.

In Bill's case, once Bill saw Frank wasn't interested in
fishing, he thought of him as being just an ordinary boss, which

Frank certainly wasn't. And when Bill grabbed Jimmy by the hair of his head and jerked him around, Bill made an enemy of Frank. Bill knew that well by the end of the school year.

On the other hand, Bill and others knew Jessica Morgan, a new teacher, was a favorite of Frank's. Jessica knew he had his eye on a Persian rug for her, something she needed for her new apartment. Jessica boasted about that.

If Frank knew Sted had gone at the crack of dawn to the dock to retrieve the larger tarp there, carrying it, still in its wrappings, to the hay room, he might have wondered why Sted did that, but he wouldn't have worried about it. He had no idea Sted disliked him. In the hay room, Sted put the tarp on a shelf and removed the large, heart-shaped rock from the window sill. He placed that rock on a bale of hay, covering it with some of the hay.

Frank was surprised when he got a phone call from Stedman Robbins.

"Well, I'm sorry to say I don't have a use for this gorgeous rug, and I can't see leaving it where it is. It'll just go to ruin. Are you still wanting it?"

"I might be. Just how much do you want for it?"

"Not a thing. Why Dalt and Tim put it into the hay room, I can't guess. You just need to come get it."

"When?" Sted could tell from the voice that Frank was eager.

"You could come get it right now if you want to. I'm pretty busy with all the books here at the house these days. I need to take a break, take a walk. You could come up the service road. You'll see me waiting outside the hay room. You'll just have to help put it into your car or your trunk. Then away you'll go, and I can take my walk."

"I'm on my way, then." Frank told his wife he had to go out, but he didn't tell her where he was going since the rug wasn't a gift for her. He did call Jessica, though, so she'd be home to receive the gift.

Sted was outside the hay room, wearing his oldest, most comfortable jeans, a tee shirt, good walking shoes, and was holding a walking stick. There was no Nell or Tim at the cottage this day. As for Dalt, Bill, and Ricky, they were fishing, and, if he knew Dalt, he probably had moved them away from the cottage farther away on the lake, away from the dock. He'd said he wanted to take a walk rather than fish today, causing Ricky to give him a questioning look. It was getting along late afternoon, and Lela and her quarrelsome dog had already gone. Any noise Sted made would be unnoticed.

It was amazing, he thought, how trusting people were once you knew what motivated them. The desire to be pleased, to be praised—that was powerful. And so he smiled when Frank's car came up the service road and stopped near the spot where he stood.

"Won't take a minute. Come help me bring it out."

Frank said nothing. He entered the hay room without a word and saw the rug, rolled up and standing in the corner.

"There may be a torn place. I'm sorry about that. If you look on the far side, see if you see what I spotted."

"Oh, no," Frank muttered. He could see his big reward for Jessica slipping away. He advanced to the rug, turning himself a little, prepared to inspect it.

Sted reached for the rock and took it in hand. The first blow struck Frank on the left side of his skull, staggering him, and knocking him off balance. Once Frank's head was lower than Sted's waist, it was in a good position for Sted to rain blow after blow so that Frank slid a little closer and closer to the floor with each blow. Frank ended up with a crushed skull, lying on the floor, dying.

"Give my boy trouble?" Sted said calmly to him. "See what that got you."

Frank was large but not so heavy as one would imagine,

80

being mostly fat and water, not muscle. Sted had no problem getting him to the trunk of his car once he located the keys from the hay room floor where they'd fallen. He folded both Frank and the rug into the trunk. Sted put the large tarp on the passenger seat.

He drove Frank's car into the woods northward on the service road till it narrowed and became a weedy hiking road. On the right, a natural wall, granite and slate, rose up, and on the left, the terrain became wild gullies and ravines shaded by trees.

Sted turned left, the car lurching over the rocky surface, its sides and underside slapped by weeds and rocks, till it suddenly pitched forward into a deep ravine, one that sloped gently upward at its bottom, allowing the car to roll forward, level enough for Sted to get out. He knew from previous walks, when he'd explored its size and shape, that no vehicle could be seen from the road and that beyond, there was nothing but rocks strewn all over what had once been a service road. There was no outlet on its northern end.

Frank and the folded rug were left in the trunk. Sted took the tarp and unfurled it, using it to cover the car. The tarp was so large it completely covered all with plenty of room to spare. There would be snows and dropping of leaves, helping to disguise the car. He felt sure it would be quite some time before it was discovered.

He walked back to the cottage, arriving just before dusk turned to darkness. He took the time to gather up any bloodied hay on the floor, dumping all that over the fence on the other side of the service road into the meadow. He used a couple of buckets of water from the tack room to flush blood from the hay room floor and covered that area with new hay. Then he took a quick shower in the tack room, washing off the rock as well as himself. He put the rock back on the window sill where it usually was to be found. He changed into the clean clothes he'd stashed in the

81

tack room earlier, and he went to the side of the hay room, to a hole he'd started, putting those possibly bloodied clothes in it, pushing them so they were actually under the building. He scooped soil over the hole with his hands, tamping the dirt down to be sure the items were covered. He'd accomplished much in about four and a half hours.

He entered the house through the kitchen, stopping to wash his hands at the sink. Dalt had eaten dinner, but he'd saved some for Sted. Bill and Ricky were gone. He found Dalt on the porch, and there he ate, hearing there were no fish biting. It was too late in the day, Dalt said. It was amazing how soundly Sted slept that night.

Jessica Morgan was alarmed when no Frankie and no rug appeared. Days later, she got a phone call from Frank's wife, wondering if she knew his whereabouts. Eventually, the wife called the police.

For the second time, Chief Don Axel came to question Sted. He was suspicious now, and it showed on his face. Sted admitted he got the rug just to spite Wilkes. He said he tossed it into the trench Tim dug out of meanness but had it taken out when Dalt and Tim objected to doing that to it. And wasn't that right, Dalt?

Don noticed that Dalt met his eyes head-on, affirming Sted's story.

And then, Sted said, he decided to contact Wilkes and offer him the rug.

Frank Wilkes came and got the rug, Sted said. He helped put it into the trunk of the car, and then Frank drove off, turning around and going out the service road the way he came, back to the county paved road.

No, he didn't notice which way he went when he got to the paved road. He was turned around by then, headed for a relaxing walk into the woods. Did anyone see him giving the rug to

Wilkes? He didn't think so, not that he knew of. Why did he decide so suddenly to give Wilkes the rug? He didn't know. He just decided to, that's all. Why did Wilkes want the rug in the first place? He had no idea. Don noticed Dalt was looking away, studying his fingernails as if he suddenly noticed he had a hang nail.

Sted obliged Axel and led him to the hay room. He'd taken an afternoon's time to scrub and bleach and air out and re-cover with hay. It looked just fine in there.

People were puzzled. Where could Frank have gone, then? And why?

The next time Tim came to work, he saw the dock was clear, but in the hay room now there were two newer tarps. And there were those two anchors, definitely not the same two anchors as those that had been on the dock. The big heart-shaped rock he'd previously put in a prominent place on the window sill was there, but now it was on the opposite side, not in the same place as before.

But nobody questioned Tim. He left, shaking his head.

Part of what Sted said was true. He did put the rug, folded, into the trunk of Frank Wilkes's car. Nobody asked if he also folded Frank up and put him in there, too.

10

A Surprise for Nell and a Mistake

Jimmy Stevens and Frank Wilkes had been easy. But now Sted had some cautious thoughts about being a protector. It could be risky.

He was sure of a couple of things about Tom Lawson, but there were dangers. For example. He knew Tom loved his mother, Nell, and he knew she loved her son, Tom. Yet, on the other hand, Tom was a huge fellow, as strong as he was big. He was armed, usually, seldom alone in his car, and often was followed around by another car. So it might take some doing, this one would.

Tom saw himself as a financial help for Nell and Tim, but the fact he was selling drugs prevented that; Nell would take no money from him. Nell had her Tom figured wrong, though, for Tom wasn't one of those suppliers who had to sell drugs to take care of their own addictions. Tom wasn't a drug user. The way he saw it, the suppliers weren't the problem. If there weren't users, there wouldn't be suppliers.

He knew about users. In a small place like Conshe Mountain, even here there were users, and some of them were folks who owned things and ran things. Tom saw them as losers on their way out. However, he wasn't a hater. Genuine people, white or black, those who didn't use, but didn't judge Tom, either, got his respect, even his affection. He liked Ricky, because Ricky hired whites and blacks and was an easy boss to work for. He liked Dalt because his mother, Nell, was so fond of him, and she was so well paid and well treated. Most of all, he liked Sted. He gave to the same charities Tom so often did, and Sted did so quietly, not caring for praise. Furthermore, Nell had told him Sted was a man of sorrows, a man who hadn't had much of a dad or mom, and Tom, who never knew his father, felt sympathy about that.

If Tom could have seen Sted's rage after he woke from a dream in which he saw his "son" Bill turned into some sort of zombie because of drugs Tom gave to him, he might have changed his mind about Sted. Or been afraid of him.

It took Tom by surprise when one of the men who worked for Ricky told him Sted would like a phone call from Tom on a matter of importance concerning Nell. That very day at noon, Tom called.

Sted went directly to the point. There were books soon going to the auction block, and Nell knew about that. She was aware the sale of those books would bring a lot of money into Sted's house. She expected nothing. That was what Sted respected so much about Nell. He intended, at the final tallying, to give Nell a lot of that money, some thousands of it. But he wanted it to be a complete surprise for her. She had done so much for Dalt and him; she certainly deserved that and more.

To be sure she would be surprised, Sted had a plan. He had three British naval law books, first editions, undoubtedly worth hundreds, sitting on a windowsill in his bedroom. He would give those three books to Tom, and Tom would give one to Nell, one to Tim, and keep one himself. Nell would be so pleased, and she would think that was it, all she was going to get.

Tom had to swear he wouldn't let slip that she was to get more than just that. And he was to come pick up the books pretty soon so that no error could be made, because those books, by mistake, might be sent out to auction with all the rest.

It would be a simple matter, easy to do. Come on the county paved road right up to the service road. Tom wouldn't even have to drive up the service road. Just give Sted a call as Tom was leaving to come there—Sted gave him the number—and Sted would walk down the road with the books. He had a car he was going to wash in the garage, and then after, Sted would be able to take his walk, so come before dark. And tomorrow afternoon was the best time to come, for that book appraiser was coming very soon. How's about it, then?

Tom was so easy. He was trusting.

Sted had pondered on it, how to be out there and be sure Tom would allow him to come close, be relaxed.

When Tom got to the service road, he saw a smiling Sted standing there in a misting rain; a raincoat draped over his shoulders. His right arm was in a cast with a wide sling supporting it. His left arm held the three books pressed against his side. Tom pulled into the service road, rolled his window down, and Sted approached.

Sted noticed there was a female passenger, just one, and there was no car on the road behind Tom's car.

"What happened to you?" Tom asked, smiling. Sted stood by the window.

"I took a hard fall," Sted said, and he lifted the three books over the window sill in such a way one of the three fell out of the crook of his arm into the car and into Tom's lap.

Tom's attention was drawn immediately downward. The first shot that came from the gun concealed in the fake cast blasted away the material that had concealed it and entered the left side of Tom's head. The second shot caught Tom's female passenger full in the face. Two more shots, one in the head of each victim, satisfied Sted they were dead or dying.

If there had been another passenger or a second car, he would have done nothing except give the books. But now the thing was done, and he intended to work quickly in case a car came along on the county road. He had figured there might be a passenger, and there was no way he could push Tom's body over so he could drive the car. He'd thought of a simple plan if that were the case, and now he fished out some heavy rope from behind the meadow fence. He took off the cast and sling and tossed those into the back seat. He managed to tumble Tom's heavy body out of the car into the road, where it lay face up. He looked in the car and on the road till he found all four of the spent bullet casings. He tied the heavy rope to Tom's feet, and then, leaving very little slack line, he tied the rope to the car bumper. Tom's feet were almost under the car, and now Sted drove up the service road to the hay room, dragging Tom's body along slowly. He left the three books there, temporarily, in the hay room.

He knew he was damn lucky no cars came up that road while he was doing all that.

That whole process was risky. Someone passing on the paved road would see what was going on, but he wanted to be well away from the house so no shots would be heard. Lela, Bill, and Dalt were working on the books inside the house, and Ricky could be sitting on the porch or fishing in the shallows, and if one of them came to the service road, they could see, also. But his luck held, and after he left the books, he took from the hay room one of the tarps he had stashed there, placing it on the passenger side floor. Then he drove slowly up that service road, Tom's body dragging along behind.

At that certain spot marking the ravine location, he stopped. He walked to the drop-off, making sure he'd take a path that would prevent him from driving Tom's car right into Wilkes's car, and he kicked out of the way as much as he could rocks that might cause Tom's body to come loose. The car ended up where it couldn't be seen, and Tom's body was behind it, clear of it. Before he left the car for good, he took out the tarp, unbound it and spread it over the car. Even when he pulled Tom's body closer to the car bumper, the tarp didn't quite cover all of it, he was disappointed to see. Mentally, he made a note about that. He left the spent casings, the fake cast and sling there in the back seat. Then he walked back home in a rain that was beginning to come down harder. Blood on the road would be gone.

The rain that night was heavy, and Sted slept peacefully. In the morning, he cleaned the gun and put it away in its box in his closet.

Sooner or later, Tom would be missed—in this case, sooner. That was because Tom's female passenger told one of her friends they were going to Sted's place to pick up some books.

So once again, Chief Don Axel came to see Sted. This time he wasn't cordial. Tom wasn't a model citizen, but Don was beginning to think Sted might be something much worse. What did Sted think about the fact people started out for his place and then disappeared? Sted looked very unhappy at the tone of that question. He certainly hoped nobody thought he was guilty of anything.

Sted admitted he'd had a conversation with Tom. He'd asked Tom to call him. He wanted to give three books to Tom, one for him, one for Tim, and one for Nell. But when Tom called (and Sted knew they could check on calls coming in to him), Sted decided he didn't want to stand out in the rain, and he and Tom agreed he would give the three books to Ricky. Then Tom could pick them up from Ricky's shop, or Tim could take them home with him.

"So Tom never came up the service road?"

"No, we arranged for me to give the books to Ricky."

"And did you?"

"No, I didn't have time to do that yet.

He was asked to produce the books, which he did, and Don noticed and read a thank-you note for Nell in one of the books. He was also asked if he had a gun. Sted had to produce the gun and let Don have it for a while to test it.

"Have you ever fired this gun?"

"I always take it with me when I go for walks in the woods. Yes, I've shot it, mostly at feral dogs or coyotes I see in the woods. I shot it at some feral dogs the last time I went walking, as a matter of fact. I think they were dogs, at least."

And that was it. Eventually, Sted got his gun back from the mayor.

Sted once again became a cheerful and peaceful man, at least he was until he had dreams featuring Jessica Morgan.

Chief of Police Don Axel came from his meeting with Mayor Dick Letterer and the City Council feeling frustrated. His brother Greg was partly to blame for that. Greg worked in the town's business office, and he and a few other employees had held a meeting with Sted recently. A couple of agencies were coming up short. Good old Sted was making things healthy again with donations, as he had once before, so no one had to be laid off, and no agency had to cut back. And, most importantly, there didn't have to be meetings about taxes. Greg just couldn't say enough about Sted, all of it good.

That popularity of Sted's was part of the problem, as far as Don was concerned. For example, some thought Dalt was a peculiar man, but Don didn't. Dalt came into town to get groceries and things he needed to keep that cottage in good repair. He was friendly but sort of shy, a strikingly handsome man even though he was older. The way women ran to him was the only bad thing people could say about Dalt.

Sted was a different thing. He smiled too much, inquired about your health, shook your hand too vigorously, and yet his eyes were empty. It set off alarm bells every time Don had to deal with Sted.

Life, Don thought, was like a long letter that came in the mail. The gist of it all was there in the middle, and all the rest at the beginning and the end was just to confuse you. Sted was like that. He was like that long letter with something hidden in the middle. Don's protective instincts, the way he wanted to protect the little town in which he was born, practically growled when he came near Sted.

The mayor and the council didn't want to listen to Don when he said he wanted to investigate that service road on Sted's property. People were disappearing, but nobody wanted to hear anything of it. Sted might not like it, they said. Do what you must, but don't disturb or upset Sted. Don left the meeting gritting his teeth.

At one time, Sted's property over on the other side of the lake provided work for a lot of people who arrived at the kitchen every morning for years. Now, there was just Nell and Tim and Dalt and Sted, and, of course, landscapers who had to help with the outside because it was so extensive. And, of course, there was that angel, which, Don had to admit, gave him the creeps.

He was angry enough that he drove on the county road to the entrance at the back of Sted's property, that dirt service road. He turned his patrol car and drove up it, deliberately trespassing, not much caring if anyone saw him. He passed the buildings on his right, the meadow on his left, and continued going north on it, glimpsing part of the property that faced the lake, the driveway nobody used because it wandered for miles around the lake. He knew Dalt had the service road graded each year, and for a while, it was a pleasant drive, till it suddenly became nothing more than a wide hiking trail full of weeds, and then, just as suddenly, it was full of rocks and ledges, with gullies and tree-shaded ravines all around. Ahead, he could see nothing but rocks and growth. There was no outlet. It was a dead end. He managed to turn around, and he felt disappointment as he drove out.

He sought out John Hershel, a retired former chief of police. Hershel lived quietly, but he still thought like a cop. "It's going to take a search warrant for that property," Don said. "Something's very wrong there."

"You'll have to have a damn good reason to get one," John told him. "Lots of people are afraid Sted might move away or just stop giving or caring any more."

"I don't think he really cares, anyway. That's what my gut tells me about him. John, first we have that runaway Stevens kid, and I hear trespassing over there at night was big with him, and suddenly he's gone. Then there's Wilkes, and he's on his way there, and he's gone. Then, Nell Lawson's son Tom, and I understand he was going there for some books, and he's gone. Mighty funny."

"Anything to go on?"

"No, nothing."

"Have you talked to Stedman?"

"Yes, and he's slick, has answers for everything."

"Then you're stuck."

"When do we act, then? When buzzards are circling?"

91

"He'll make a mistake. The slickest ones always do."

It was a very short visit. When he left, Don looked skyward. He didn't see any buzzards.

He would have been impressed if he could have seen the larger tarp put over Tom's body and the stones holding it in place. Working in the woods at night was no problem for Sted.

The dream about Jessica Morgan was the worst. It filled Sted with disgust. She was seducing a youthful Bill, but she had the poor boy tied up, and Sted woke up spluttering. "Whore! Whore!" he cried out as he threw off his bed covers and fled from his bedroom.

As for the real Jessica Morgan, she was perplexed when Sted called her. She asked right away about Frank and the rug.

"I'm surprised you haven't heard from him," Sted told her. "He left here with the rug. I put it in the trunk of his car myself. This is so disturbing. I'm sorry he's missing. It's frightening."

Well, then, she wanted to know why in the world was he calling her. It's quite a story, he said.

"We're organizing all the books over here to send them off. And, well, as an English teacher, I bet you know the value of a first edition Charles and Mary Lamb, a telling of three Shakespearean tragedies. There's such a book here, and it's got a personal note penned on a page at the back. That might add to its value a bit. I figure the book must be worth hundreds. If you're interested in it, I'll give it to you, free, of course. You'll have to come get it, though, because I'm way too busy helping catalog all the books. If you would like it, just give me a call, choose any day, and then just come during the day. Let me meet you at the kitchen entrance, on the service road. I'll give you the book, and you'll drive off, and then I can take a walk to have a break from all those books."

There was silence on the line. "Since it's worth money, I wouldn't want to give it to anyone else. Lela has given me the name of a book collector in New York, and I'll pass that card on to you, in case later on you want to sell it."

Silence. "Of course, I thought of you at once. Frank always said so many complimentary things about you and your teaching. It shouldn't go to anyone else."

She finally said she would see what she could do about it.

A few days later, she did call, and Sted stood outside the hay room, waiting for her car to arrive. He enjoyed the sun, dressed in baggy walking shorts and a tee shirt. He wasn't surprised to see there were three women in the car. Jessica, not entirely trusting Sted, brought a couple of women friends with her, just as he thought she probably would.

One of the strange things about the books found in his father's collection was the fact that sometimes there was more than one copy of a particular book. In this case, there were not just one or two, but several copies of the Lamb book. Amazing. And it was to come in so handy. He approached Jessica's car with a big welcoming grin. "Oh, my! What have we here? A car full of beauties!"

Sted wasn't the Hollywood handsome Dalt was, but his curly hair, touched with silver at the temples, and his dark eyes that sparkled when he was excited brought responses from women, and he knew it. He and Dalt were alike in that they were still physically sound and strong. There was nothing overweight about either of them. The women all giggled and smiled back.

"It's a happy coincidence that's developed here today! Jessica, I was going to give you all the copies, but this is even better, for we can share, one for each of you. Only one has the penned message in the back, but all are valuable. We found other copies of the same book, same year and edition only this morning! I have that book collector's name and phone and address written down, and you can share that info. Just sit tight, and I'll get those books. I put them in the hay room earlier." As he turned away, he glanced at Jessica's lovely face. She was a very pretty woman with petulant lips (his aunt Eva would have described her as "somebody's science project", for her good looks were planned and accomplished through heavy effort). The quickest look, and he could see she was thinking she could have had all the books if only she had come alone.

He returned with three books. The fourth, the last one, was left sitting on a hay bale. He deliberately gave the special one, the one in which there was a message penned on one of its back pages, to one of the three women who was not Jessica. Two of the women rode away chatting and happy. Jessica wasn't smiling.

He let a week pass. He called Jessica again.

"We're almost done with all the books, and guess what. There's one more copy of that book. The thought came to me that you haven't been treated very well. I feel guilty about how I distributed those three books. I should have given them all to you as I planned to in the first place. You were disappointed about the rug, and then I went and disappointed you about the books. Please forgive me. So… as a pleasant surprise, there's more. I have been thinking about giving away some of my mother's jewelry. Can't bring myself to sell any of it, but I want to give some pieces to women she knew and to a few others here in Conshe. I think you'd love her aquamarine ring. It's an exquisite and expensive piece, and I would gladly pay one of our local jewelers to have it made to fit you if it doesn't already. Think you would like to look at it?"

There was that silence again. "If you haven't the time to look at it, or aren't interested, perhaps you can recommend some other English teacher. It's just that Frank Wilkes said so many complimentary things about you, I thought of you at once, as soon as I made a decision about it. Once again, you can pick your day and time, but I can't bring it to you. I'm stuck here till that appraiser comes and goes."

There wasn't any problem with Jessica this time. She agreed she would come, and was so eager she wanted to come to the hay room the following morning. He put her off, claiming he would be very busy during the morning, but mid-afternoon would be perfect. He'd need a break by then, anyway.

It was dangerous, very dangerous, but he didn't care. He wanted this to be over. When he saw her car turning onto the service road, he moved toward her, walking just a little down the road, holding the one book and the little blue box that contained the aquamarine so that she could see both.

She rolled her window down. He had marveled before about how strange it is that people feel safe if they're in a car with the window rolled down, even when they're in danger. That thought came to him again. He handed her the book, and she gushed her thanks for it, but her eyes were fixed on that little blue box. When he gave it to her, she took the box into her lap, and she was looking downward. Sted slipped the gun from behind his back, out of the waistband of his pants. He shot her once in the head. And that was that.

True, Tim or Nell, or anybody could have come along, but nobody did. Sted's luck held, and he got the anchors and the last tarps out and onto the floor of the passenger side of the car. He pushed her slender body over into the passenger seat, and after he located the spent shell casing and the blue box, he took over as the driver.

Before he reached that spot where he would turn into the deep chasm where the car would be left, he shot Jessica again to be sure she really was gone, and he made sure both spent casings were in the car. The blue box he put in his pocket. He took the last book from the car and used one tarp to cover, yet again, one more time, Tom's body, for there certainly was beginning to be a smell. Gagging, he tucked the new tarp around it all as best he could, and then he put the two anchors on top of that newest tarp. He looked skyward; he'd been worried about buzzards circling, but he didn't see any.

The last thing he did was cover up Jessica's car with the last tarp in his possession.

He walked back to the cottage feeling like a conquering hero. She was Circe, who turned men into animals, and he had overcome her; that's how he saw it.

For little Bill, school would start again pretty soon, and there would be no Jimmy, no Frankie, no Tom, and no Jessica to make life difficult.

Sted would have felt differently if he'd realized he made a mistake. Jessica did indeed have the blue box open, and the ring was in her hands when he shot her. When he pulled her body slightly out of the car so he could jam in the anchors and tarps, just before he pushed her body back in and over to the passenger side, the ring fell out of the car. The blue box snapped shut and stayed in the car, falling to the floor, but the ring wasn't in it. The ring was lying in the dirt of the service road. Sted had made the one mistake John Hershel had predicted.

While Sted was still sleeping, Dalt sat on the front porch with his cup of coffee. He thought of Tim's complaints. From where he sat in the faint light of dawn, he certainly could see the dock was clear—no tarps, no anchors.

He, being Dalt, decided to go see what might be in the hay room. He walked through the house to the kitchen, out the kitchen door, and down the path to the service road, sipping his coffee as he went. He remembered Tim's saying there had been one big tarp and several small ones on the dock originally, but they kept disappearing, according to Tim, until the last time Tim was working. That time, he was complaining he felt sure there were new ones, or so he thought. He felt he'd lost count, but he knew "something wasn't right." In the hay room, this time there were items lying about, but not one tarp and not any anchors, either.

As Dalt turned to leave, he guessed Tim would have something more to say when next he came.

And then he saw the ring lying in the dirt.

Every time she wore it, people noticed it, and quite a few wished they owned it. It cost thousands, of course, with diamonds surrounding it in its setting.

There was no doubt it was Helen's large, exquisite aquamarine. Helen said she liked to wear it, especially in the winter, when it reminded her of summer skies. Then she always felt she had something of summer with her.

He cleaned the ring, and later, when Sted was working on the books Bill found, Dalt looked into Sted's room. Once, it had been Helen's room. She always kept that blue ring box on her dresser. Dalt saw it now, sitting there, open. So Sted must know the ring was missing. He put the ring back into its box and closed it. He wondered, of course, how something Helen loved so much could end up lying in the dirt, and he made a little vow to himself to go seek out Sted next time he went off into the woods by himself.

A scowling Don Axel came calling again. "Her teacher friends say they came up that service road, and you gave them books."

Sted admitted he did. And yet, he said, there was one more book, so he called Jessica Morgan and asked her if she wanted it. She didn't respond, so he called her again and asked if there was some other teacher of English she might know who would want it. She didn't know of anyone, but then she asked if he was going to sell any of his mother's jewelry. She would be interested in that if he was going to. He wasn't going to, so that was the end of their communication.

Don could tell, just from looking at Dalt, there was something seriously untrue in this story. He wasn't sure what it was, but it must be a big mistake, for he could tell Dalt knew something.

He played on that. "You know what, Sted? I don't believe you. You're a liar."

Of course, with lowered eyelids, Sted put on an offended air. Don wasn't watching him. Instead, he gave Dalt a sideways look. Dalt visibly flinched when Don called Sted a liar, but he remained silent. He was looking away, not willing to look Don in the eye.

Don's spirits rose. As he left, he thought to himself, *I've got you now. You've made a mistake, and Dalt knows what it is. Sooner or later, I'll know what it is, too.* He felt like humming a tune; the future was so clear to him.

11

A Forgotten Page

Eventually, Lela called an antique dealer in New York, and that person put her in touch with somebody else, another dealer who specialized in fine antiques and collectible books. After that, in some way word got around that Reginald Robbins's library was going to be examined.

The phone in the kitchen rang one morning, and when Sted answered it, a voice with just a tinge of a British accent identified himself as Thomas Leeghes, a descendant of one of the families who were the founders and workers of Sotheby's auction house in London during the 1700s. He wondered if he could examine the books.

For a moment, Sted hesitated. "You say you're connected to Sotheby's in London? Why would you be calling here? Isn't there a Sotheby's in New York? I don't understand."

There was a pause at the other end. "Your father and mother were born in England, Mr. Robbins. They migrated to America and became naturalized citizens. Originally, their home was in Somerset. Mr. Robbins's niece, daughter of his sister, Ann, is still alive there. I think Ann's son was killed in the war, though, so you're probably the last male of that line. My father knew your father's family and also knew him through his purchases, particularly his books on British naval affairs. Your auction would, of course, be in America."

Sted was startled. "I didn't know that about my parents. Are you calling me from London?"

"I'm in New York at the moment. My mother is American, so I travel back and forth. Usually I'm in England, but I've come to New York hoping I can travel to Pennsylvania and have the chance to see the books I've heard about. Would you consider letting me have a look?"

Dalt was sitting nearby, and he could hear the conversation, at least Sted's end of it. He was surprised when Sted readily agreed.

"Certainly. Give us a week to make sure things are in order here, then give us a call, and come ahead. We're a bit removed from the nearest town, so you can stay here, if you don't mind books piled in your bedroom. Or, if you prefer staying in the town, we could arrange to come get you and take you back each day. Decide on that after you get here. How would you charge a fee?"

"Let me see what has to be done first; how many books, that sort of thing. I'll keep it very reasonable because I'm anxious to be the only one working on them. Sotheby's to be the auction house."

When he hung up, Sted looked at Dalt with an astonished expression on his face. "Dalt, both my parents were born in England. The man who called is from Sotheby's auction house, and he wants to come see the books. I've told him to come ahead. Are you impressed?"

"I'm remembering things your mother had… some sort of standing lion coat of arms. We'll have to get Nell and Tim here on a daily basis while he's here. What's his name?"

That remained a mystery since Sted didn't remember it. But

soon enough, Sted heard from the man again.

Early on a still morning that late summer, Dalt and Ricky were sitting on the porch. Sted, Nell and Tim were in the kitchen, and Lela and her dog were still finishing one last pile or two of books, running about to put them in the proper piles. Bill was with Lela, determined they would be completely finished before anybody arrived.

Ricky had driven the Buick, wanting to show it off. He took the long way around the lake, turning at last where brick pillars announced the Robbins' driveway, and then he enjoyed yet another mile of driving to finally park his Buick right at the foot of the long front porch steps. The Buick was almost completely finished now, and it was his statement of the quality and completeness of what he did for a living. He wanted it parked where the hot shot Brit would see it, along with anybody else who might be hoity-toity high class.

Leeghes was one tired man. He had flown from London to New York, and then to Pittsburgh without much rest, and now the driver of the car he'd hired to get him to Conshe Mountain and the cottage got confused and lost for a little while until he saw the pillars marking the entrance to the property. Now, as Thomas Leeghes stepped out from the car, he gave the driver a generous tip and gathered the small traveling bag under his arm. He waited for the driver to fish out his two suitcases. As he did that, he got a good look at the old Buick, and those on the porch got a good look at him.

He was not a skinny man. He was of medium height but a little overweight. What's more, he didn't dress as they might have expected. "Rumpled" might best describe him. They expected someone who might look British. The man they saw could have come from Brooklyn. However, he had about him an air of confidence, and Ricky could see his beloved Buick was being ogled by an eye that had seen many collectible cars on more than one continent. Ricky was sitting heads-up alert, watching this foreigner.

"Well, once I get settled, must have a look under the bonnet of this one," he called out cheerfully to those on the porch. Ricky frowned.

"Bonnet?" He looked to Dalt.

"I think he means the hood, the front." To Tim, who had come to the front door, Dalt added, "Please get Sted, and let Lela know her dog should be on the leash." Tim disappeared.

"What's he calling the back, then?" Ricky asked softly, but Leeghes heard that, obviously, for he said as he got to the porch, "That would be the boot."

Sted came out onto the porch, and they made their introductions. Tim was to get Leeghes and suitcases to a bedroom upstairs, and then, if he wanted something to eat, bring him back down to Nell. Leeghes wanted none of that. He wanted to get some sleep, he said.

Shortly after that, he ran into Ruben. There was a burst of growling and barking, and a voice crying out, "Bloody bounder!" Then Lela's voice was heard controlling the dog, so the poor man could escape to his room, probably nursing his ankle as he went there.

Ricky was fiddling with his beer can. "Somebody should warn Lela that fucker doesn't talk English."

They should have expected the unexpected from Thomas Leeghes. That night, Dalt heard such loud snoring coming from the nearby upstairs bedroom where Leeghes was sleeping, he got up from his bed and closed both the door to the bedroom where the guest slept and his own bedroom door as well.

At about four a.m., Thomas was up. He emerged from his bedroom in his pajamas, bathrobe, and slippers. He was armed with pens and legal-sized writing pads. Sniffing, snorting, and making all sorts of nasal noises, he came down the stairs and was attempting to make some tea for himself when Dalt, who was wide awake by then, came to his rescue.

The day had begun for Leeghes. Still dressed in his pajamas and robe, he worked throughout the morning, stopping to eat what Nell fixed for him, to make a few phone calls, and to go to the bathroom. Shamelessly, Bill and Lela tried to follow him about, hoping perhaps to engage him in conversation, but they soon saw there was no chance of that.

He ate lunch silently. He spent his time for the next week and a half in that fashion, his glasses perched on the end of his nose, taking notes, inspecting books, writing mysterious things, and making phone calls. If they expected he would join them for dinner each evening, full of wonderful conversation, they were to be disappointed. He did get dressed each day, somewhere around noon, and he walked about the garden, even there with a book in hand. He might join them for dinner... or perhaps not. When he did talk with them, he was friendly and warm, but his attention was on the books, not on the people.

He talked with Nell and Tim more than any of the others. He was curious about the angel in the garden, and everyone, including Sted, who sat rigidly listening, heard Nell explain the statue to him in the simplest terms.

And, then, just when they began to wonder if he would ever be done, he suddenly was. He announced one morning he would be ready to give them his report that evening.

Everyone was sitting at the big round table in the common

room. They always sat there to eat sandwiches, play cards, or eat their supper, ignoring the dining room. They'd eaten earlier, and now they waited till Leeghes finished eating in the kitchen and walked out to where they sat. Nell and Tim lingered in the kitchen, also listening. Sted sat in the big rocker by the fireplace.

Thomas Leeghes looked like a tourist this evening. He wore loafers, no socks, an open collared shirt, and casual slacks. He brought with him his notes and a stack of papers he put on the table in case he needed to refer to them. They felt this was a man who bought expensive clothes but wore them till they were threadbare if he liked them. They could sense he knew so much about books he didn't need "style" to bolster his confidence. There was complete silence around the table.

He sat down in the last available chair at the table. "I know you're all interested in my findings. It was even better than I'd heard. You have to realize what these books get depends on who the people are that I can bring to the auction. Stedman, I've never seen more impressive books on British naval history than are right here in this house. It's my impression, just a guess, that your father's family must have had a connection to the British navy. The books he chose are, in some cases, irreplaceable. They are the very last and so are more attractive to British buyers. It would be too costly to send all these books to the London auction. But individually, they can be sent safely if offers come in from London during the auction or even ahead of it. I'll make contact with those I know will be interested.

"I expected to be impressed by the naval books. Your father left close to eight hundred of them. Of those, at least two hundred are treasures. Among them are three volumes, first edition, entitled *Naval and Military Memoirs*. They're in fine condition even though they are so very old, and I'm getting phone inquiries on them already. There are two books, 1800s, on *Naval Tactics* and *British Points of Seamanship*, that I think should bring at least three thousand each. There's a little thing, *Two Years at Sea*, 1834, in very bad condition, but it's charming. I would like to keep that item myself.

"A couple of books by a Captain Ross, on the Atlantic and two of his ships are interesting in spite of their poor condition. What is bringing a lot of phone calls are two volumes on Nelson. One of those is love letters from him to Lady Emma Hamilton, and bidding might start high on that.

"But I never expected so many things that don't pertain to Britain's navy at all. Stedman, you have four books on philosophy and philosophers with exquisite leather bindings in spite of their age. Don't include them in this auction, please. Let me give you contacts for private parties. At auction, they won't bring as much as they will if offered privately.

"I was taken with *The Lewis and Clark Expedition* that Bill is holding there. Despite its condition, I estimate it would bring thousands at auction, perhaps as much as fifteen or twenty thousand. You also have that Patrick Gass journal, 1807, first edition, with its long title on the Lewis and Clark expedition. I think that could bring almost as much."

Every now and then, Thomas would look around the table at everyone, as if congratulating them.

"You have a Dickens 1835 first edition *Pickwick Papers* with nearly perfect leather binding, and a five-volume set of his works. Unbelievable.

"Of great interest to several people I know is this one, *A Dictionary of the English Language*, by Samuel Johnson, first edition, 1755. And, of all things, a United Kingdom first edition, 1791, *The American Revolution*.

"*And* you have two volumes, *The Personal Memoirs of Ulysses S. Grant*. First editions, which I also find interesting.

"The one that takes my breath away is this one. I haven't seen a complete set like this one in my lifetime. Your father, Stedman, must have picked these books up as he found them here and there over his lifetime. It is *The Complete Works of Edgar Allan Poe*, all seventeen volumes. I already have phone inquiries on this one, so the bidding might start high, and I've no idea how much it would bring. I was impressed with it, to put it mildly."

At this point, Nell brought him a small pot of tea, and he poured himself a cup. He looked supremely happy, as if he could see Sotheby's making a lot of money from what he'd found.

"I found one other thing in this house I would never have thought to find here. Dalt tipped me off about it. In a closet in your room, Sted, wrapped in cotton material, you have an illuminated parchment."

Ricky whispered to Dalt, "Illuminated?"

Lela smiled. "There's decorated capital letters to begin each page."

Thomas nodded. "This one is hand lettered, of course, and most elaborately illustrated and decorated. It appears to me to be a Bible made for a knight and his lady. Not only is it in good condition, but it's complete. My God, we never find these codices intact, much less complete. People bid desperately for single pages.

"For this to be in such condition, it must have been lovingly kept. It's my opinion it comes from your family, possibly your mother's family. This is my advice: keep it out of this auction. If you do want to let it go, let it go up for bid at a later auction when there are other such offerings. Its price is something I can't even guess. Stedman, if this were in a monastery, it would be chained to a table.

"Now, speaking conservatively, I can see these books bringing close to a million. Not all of that would go to you, Stedman, for Sotheby's takes its considerable cut, and there is the cost of getting the books to auction in New York, plus travel expenses for me and the people who come to transport the books. However, your final check could be in the hundreds of thousands if my guess is right. Now, before I leave, I'll give you the complete listing of all the books and all the information I have about them. If there's a volume or two or more, those you don't want sent to auction, you must tell me that as soon as possible and pull those volumes out. Now, is there anything else?"

"Yes," Sted spoke up. "Are you leaving right away?"

"Tomorrow, early as possible. There's no reason to linger."

"Then there's the matter of your personal fee. Can you tell me what that is, so I can pay you before you leave?"

"Just give me the two volumes on Grant. And the little book about life at sea. I'd count that as five thousand."

"Done. You take them with you."

"There is one other thing. At first, I didn't think your father kept any records on these books. But these pages here are what I found, also in that closet I mentioned. On these pages, in his handwriting, you can see he kept a meticulous record of everything he bought. I did find something in the middle of all that. It looks as if there's a page from a letter he'd written and then lost in the midst of all those other pages, sort of as if it's one page left out of a letter to be mailed. I've read it, of course, and here it is." He took the folded page off the top of the stack of pages he'd brought with him and handed it to Sted.

Sted read it. Then he handed it to Dalt, who also read it, and then, because Sted didn't seem to mind, the others read it, too:

107

"... cold as we had it after father's death. It's most sad here now, for Helen's not improving. There's no word from Sted, and I'm sure he must be dead. That hurt is deeper for me than for anyone else, for if I could have foreseen what would happen, perhaps I could have made sure ..."

The page was not expressing a complete thought at either end of itself. Sted sat in the rocker saying nothing for a long time after he read it. He stood up eventually, and put the page on the fireplace mantel.

Finally, Sted said, loud enough to be heard, "We'll meet here in the morning. Please, any of you, bring any book or books you want to keep."

Lela had left the room, knowing where the Grant books were, and now she returned with them, Leeghes waved at her the small book he'd already kept. She offered the Grant books to Sted, but he pointed, and she handed them over to Leeghes.

"I hope I get to see you before you go off, Thomas. Dalt's our early riser here. I'll ask him to get me up early."

Sted sent Dalt his wake-up message with his eyes, and then he disappeared into his room. Thomas Leeghes, doubtless pleased with himself, had Tim bring him a beer and a sandwich, and then he went to bed, carrying his books with him. He would pack the three books in with his belongings.

When most of the others were gone, Dalt and Lela (with her dog), sat in wicker chairs on the side porch. They could hear Nell and Tim finishing up in the kitchen. After this night, those two would go back to their Wednesday-Thursday schedule.

Ricky and Bill, driving in style in the old Buick, had already left after having supper with the others.

"Is your car here, out front?" Dalt asked Lela, for he didn't want her parking out back on the service road. It was too dark out there, and it unsettled him every time he got near it these days.

"I'm here in front, and I have plenty of time to sit and talk a while."

Oh? Dalt dared to hope. "Listen, why don't you just spend the night here?"

Then he hastened to add, "There's extra bedrooms, you know. Even with Mr. Leeghes sleeping in one of them."

At first, Lela didn't say anything. Then, she said primly, much to Dalt's surprise, "Dalt, you already have quite a reputation with the women sleeping here overnight. I don't want to end up being just another conquest for you."

"What—" Dalt began, but he was cut off in mid-protest.

"Well, Jack's been calling so often. I've been thinking of going to Pittsburgh. And Ruben is so good with you; I'm wondering if you would take him. He's such precious company."

Dalt felt as if his head was coming off his shoulders, rising like a balloon. He was giddy with anger.

"Well, goddamn it to hell, then! So off you'd go and leave me here, and every time I looked at that dog, I'd be reminded what a loser I am! Never mind! I withdraw that breakfast invitation!"

He stalked to the door into the house, trying to keep some shred of dignity, for he felt so hurt he could cry. Suddenly, he remembered. "No, wait... come tomorrow. Sted said to bring any book from the collection you want." But then, as he left her, as he entered the house, he said in anger, "And to hell with Jack!"

Next morning, everyone met in the common room. Sted was in the same rocker he sat in the previous day. The note was still on the mantel. His face looked worn this morning, as if he'd aged.

Dalt had spent a restless night, feeling sorry for himself

about Lela for a good part of the night, and the other part, trying not to remember running down the front porch steps wearing nothing but pajama bottoms, barefoot, to discover he was part of a murder. He tried not remembering paddling with his hands, trying to get back to shore, or making coffee, trembling, trying to make things normal again. He knew some people could put things in little compartments and never think of them, but he was finding out he wasn't one of those fortunate people.

Bill Accardi was cradling the huge Lewis and Clark book. If that book could bring the kind of money mentioned, couldn't he arrange for the sale of it himself? That would be a down payment on a house. His parents could come live with him, or at least visit.

It was a Wednesday, and Nell was in the kitchen, but she wasn't in good shape mentally. Tom was missing, and she couldn't guess who might have harmed him. Lela kept looking over at Dalt, but Dalt wasn't looking at anyone, certainly not at her, and certainly not at Sted.

In all, it was a sullen bunch of people. It was a good thing Ricky was sitting on the porch, as usual.

Mr. Leeghes had already left after shaking Sted's hand in parting. Now, not used to so many people around with such early rising, Sted stood with a pen and legal pad in hand. "All right, let's get started, then. Lela, let's start with you. What book or books do you want?"

"I don't want any book," she answered. "You paid me for work I got, so I enjoyed, and that was enough. Those books were your father's, and now every one of them belongs to you. You should get all the money from the auction."

For a minute, there was silence. Then Sted asked, "How about you, Dalt?"

"No book for me, either," Dalt said, not looking at anyone.

Bill was embarrassed. "No, not any book for me either, then."

"You're sure?"

"Yes. She's right."

Sted's dark eyes turned to Lela. "You begin to remind me of someone else I used to know," he said softly.

Afterward, Dalt headed back upstairs, where he was trying to take down shelves. He wanted to get rid of them, repair the walls, and then paint them white, so the big room wouldn't be so dark and dreary.

Ricky had been hanging around for days, sensing the work was over, so maybe fishing could take over. Now, he followed Dalt up the stairs, whining.

"When will you be *done*? *Ever*? Let's go fish before it gets too hot."

"Not ready yet. Go lie down in my room. There's magazines in there. Just wait for an hour or so." Reluctantly, Ricky stepped into Dalt's bedroom through a door next to the fireplace.

As he worked, Dalt's mind centered on Lela. He was impressed by her, and he felt sorry for himself. He felt old.

He heard a soft cough, and looking around, he saw Lela herself, standing in the doorway with Ruben on his leash beside her. "I want you to know nowadays I have to go looking for him, and it's the strangest thing. He's turning up at whatever place you are. That's strange, don't you think? I have to put him on the leash all the time or he'll go—"

"I'm not taking that dog, Lela."

"I know, you told me. I'm sorry I made you mad."

"Well, we're different. I'm so much older—"

"I'm not young—" she began, but he continued, cutting her off.

"I wish now I'd hugged you back. I wish I'd kissed your hair.

111

I don't know why I didn't. Afraid to, I guess. I admit... being lonely. And not feeling that way when I'm near you. I wish ..." It seemed to him she was responding, perhaps moving a step or two closer to him.

It was at that moment Ricky stuck his hugely smiling face out from Dalt's bedroom doorway, saying in a falsetto female voice, "Hel-*lo*, Lela!"

She was startled, and she dropped the leash. She gave Dalt a hurt look and fled.

He tossed the shelf he was holding and ran after her. He didn't care who saw, who thought what. "Wait, wait, Lela! I forgot he was in there! Wait up!"

He caught up with her halfway down the stairs, on the landing. He turned her toward him, holding her by her shoulders, trying to let that become a hug.

"For God's sake, don't leave! Things are so awful! It's bad enough—"

From above, there was the sound of growling and barking and cursing. Ricky had run afoul of Ruben. There was more cursing and then Ricky's voice calling down to him, saying, "Dalt, call off your goddamned dog!"

"See?" Dalt exclaimed. "Now that dog is making people think he's mine! On top of everything else! For God's sake, don't leave me here! What would I do if you leave?"

12

Maybe
Maybe I will

There is nothing like fall arriving in mountainous country. The air changes, especially at night, when it becomes clear and colder, even as things are trying to grow in the daytime. During the day, there's a smell of crushed leaves mixed with goldenrod dust, and there are certain asters that make the base of hills look as if they're covered with a purple haze.

Dying—with leaves, at least—becomes exciting, going off in the ablest of colors, draped with brightest golds and richest reds. Because of all it is, some people stand outside, inhaling deeply, swearing they will never leave.

Sted, with his love of gardens, seemed to get that. At least, this was the time of year when he let the landscapers and gardeners loose big time. The dahlias were cut low, dug out, and set for winter in bins of sand or peat moss, not to be disturbed until next spring. Roses were cut back, and protective cones were set around their roots. Dressings of woods straw protected lily beds. Clumps of sage and butterfly weed were left with old growth crumpled over them so that in spring, new growth would come peeking out from below. Tropical and semi-tropical plants were taken into the heated greenhouse shed to live a pampered winter life. Each thing was given—or, if hardy enough, was not given—whatever it needed. Sted especially loved those things that held to the edges of the woods: the holly and evergreens in winter; the dogwood and daffodils in spring. One would think he could settle in at his cottage, satisfied he was able to protect his garden, at least, until the garden awakened again.

But for Sted, sorrow never slept for long.

There had been rain during the afternoon, so the evening was wet. Even more was needed, for it had been dry for weeks. Sted had been pulling on and stacking books for so long; now he wanted to hear no more about them. He was sick of those books. He went to bed hoping he'd sleep all night.

He didn't. Instead, he dreamed about his Aunt Eva. She was screaming at him, running after him, and he couldn't get his legs to work; he couldn't run. He woke abruptly, upset. He headed for the dining room.

The pocket doors were open. A grown-up voice greeted him. "Come in," the voice said, and it was definitely Sted's own voice speaking. "There's something you don't know." He closed the doors behind himself. There was no little boy in the dining room now. There was only Sted talking to himself.

Thomas Leeghes was as good as his word. One very large truck and one medium-sized one arrived with four people. They spent three days preparing and packing the books. The people of Conshe Mountain were impressed when those trucks rolled through town, once everybody knew what was in them and where they were going.

The bidding took off with a roar at the auction when the Poe collection was offered. The naval books didn't go for as much as had been hoped. After Sotheby's took their percentage on the first one hundred thousand and a lesser cut on the rest, Sted received a respectable check for $475,075. There were expenses taken out for Leeghes's travel and for the trucks and the people who handled the books. If not for all that, Sted's share might have reached that half million mark Leeghes thought it might.

As usual, Sted cared little for money. He gave to Conshe, and he notified certain people that he wanted them to come for breakfast, where he would let them know the auction outcome. Nell and Tim, Bill, Ricky, Lela, and Dalt looked forward to hearing how much money the books brought at the auction. Of course, they would be there for breakfast.

Ricky would be driving his cherished Buick again; it was finished and complete now. He was told by Dalt that Leeghes said the work Ricky did was grand. What Dalt didn't say was that Leeghes had added, about the Buick, "That 38 Special isn't exactly scarce, you know."

What Sted didn't tell anyone was that on the common room round table, he had put an envelope for each of them, including Nell and Tim. Each envelope had inside it a check for forty thousand dollars. Anyone else would consider giving that much money away to be a serious matter. Sted gave money away and felt it was a minor thing. He felt that way about money, perhaps because he had always had it.

Dalt, rising early, noticed the envelopes on the table, and he could see there was no envelope for him. That didn't bother him. He made coffee and was preparing to start making some breakfast. That's when he saw Sted's bedroom door was open. He looked inside and saw a rumpled, empty bed. He supposed Sted was out taking one of his walks again. Even as Bill and Ricky arrived ahead of everyone else, and as others came, too, gathering in the kitchen, Dalt thought nothing was wrong. Maybe they noticed the envelopes on the table, but out of some sort of courtesy, they held off taking them until Sted arrived. They probably wondered what was in those envelopes.

Tim and Nell came in last, and Nell was obviously frightened. "We should call the police," she said. "Dalt, he's out in the garden, and he's got a gun. I could see it in his hand. He's waving it around. He says you have to come out. He's stomping around. I should call the police," she said again. Tim was nodding his head in agreement.

"What's happening?" Ricky and Bill asked. Lela was standing still, eyes big.

Dalt headed for the front porch. The others crowded out the front door after him. "What is it, Sted?" he called down to the figure in the garden. "What's wrong?"

Sted marched rigidly to the foot of the front steps, brandishing the gun.

"Plenty. That's what."

"Are you going to shoot me? Why?"

"Maybe. Maybe I will. My boy tells me you haven't told me everything. He says I can't trust you any more."

"That's what he said?"

"Damn right."

A thought raced, swift as forked lightning, across Dalt's mind. *So. You weren't sleeping. You woke up, and you were at the kitchen window when I went down the kitchen path, sipping coffee, to the service road. Later, you knew the ring was missing. You had that ring box open. When I put the ring back in, I closed it. I should have taken sharper notice of that. So you knew I put it there; who else? That tells me what I already suspected: your little boy, at some level, is something of yourself.*

All that, but now he had to reply. "Well, he's right. I didn't tell you I found Helen's ring. I put it back in the ring box. I did all that and didn't tell you. But why was it out there lying in the dirt anyway, Sted? Your mother was so fond of that ring, and you let it end up there? Why was it out there in the first place? Were you going to give it to someone, Sted?"

"No! No, I wasn't going to do anything like that." Sted seemed confused, as if he was reaching for a good answer.

116

Finally, he looked at Bill, who had been inching closer and closer to Dalt, as if to defend him. At last, Bill stepped down one step below Dalt. Ricky was moving forward on the steps, also.

"I had to protect you," Sted said, looking at Bill. "You needed protection."

Bill protested. "I thought you understood. We agreed, I didn't and I don't need protection. You promised—"

"So what?" Sted yelled at Bill.

Now it was Ricky who moved down the front steps toward Sted. It was a brave but foolish move. "Yeah! I told you, Sted! You know, his parents are Italian!" Ricky shouted. "That's not black hair; that's *wop* hair, dammit!"

Dalt saw Sted's face change, saw the past overtake him. From an earlier time, his Aunt Eva's face, seething with rage, took over. *"You tell him, Helen! Tell him that accident was the best thing ever happened to him! She had her hooks into you, boy! It's a good thing she's dead!"* Dalt remembered holding Sted back, pulling him into the kitchen, and then into the butler's pantry because he feared Sted would hit her.

At first, nobody realized Sted had pulled the trigger and shot somebody. Sted was as startled by the sound when it happened as were the others. When Ricky started screaming, it was clear at once. "I'm shot! Goddamn it, Sted, you shot me! I'm gut shot! You bastard!"

It was Bill who told Tim to call 911, who got Nell to go get some towels to staunch the bleeding. It was Bill who decided he and Tim should help Ricky down the rest of the stairs and into the Buick because it was handy, and he knew the keys were in it. The two of them started Ricky down the steps, holding his arms, supporting him. "If I die, Sted, I'll kill you! Oh, wait, no, no, no blood in the Buick! No blood in the Buick!"

Nell paused, and then she came fearlessly to Sted. "You give me that gun," she demanded, "and you tell me where my boy

117

Tom is!"

Sted crumbled. He gave Nell the gun. "He's in the woods with the others," he said calmly, as if it were the most normal thing in the world to say.

Nell went with Tim and Bill to help with Ricky. The police got the gun from her later. Lela and Dalt were left alone with Sted.

"I was going to shoot you!" Sted said over and over, his arms crossed over his chest defensively, weeping. His face was contorted with panic and fear. He kept his face buried in Dalt's chest, listening to Dalt's comforting whispers. When police came, they had to pull him away from Dalt. Then there was nothing that could be said to comfort or help. There was no little boy ghost. There was only him.

Two people and one frightened dog were left sitting and speaking in the smallest voices. Ruben huddled as close as he could get to Lela. So, for that matter, did Dalt. She made some tea. Later, Dalt made some coffee. It was the longest day, but finally the others came back, around four thirty that afternoon. While it wasn't a sure thing Ricky would eventually recover, he had survived emergency surgery.

"He's mad at us," said Tim.

"Blood. In the Buick," Bill added.

They took the envelopes then and opened them. Would these checks be good? Could they deposit them or cash them? Lela opened her envelope, eyed the check, and read the date. "He wrote these checks two days ago. Fine." They left with mixed feelings, wanting to stay but even more strongly wanting to go.

Dalt went into Sted's room. He lay down on the bed and fell asleep. The little white dog curled up on a nearby round rug and decided he would sleep, too.

Lela slipped Dalt's shoes off, and then she opened some

closets and cupboards till she found a quilt. She covered Dalt with that. Suddenly, she felt tired, too, and she took off her own shoes and slipped under the quilt to lie down beside him on the bed. She cuddled up as close to his back as she could get to be warm. She wrapped one arm over his chest, hugging him. That woke him up. He turned to her, awake and happy that she was there. There were whisperings, and he kissed her hair. When she kissed his lips, his cheek, she tasted tears.

That was when she knew she wouldn't be moving to Pittsburgh.

Very early the next morning, Don Axel came to the cottage. He noted the car parked at the front, went up the steps to the porch, and knocked at the door. At first, nobody came, and he thought nobody was up, but then, as he peered in, he got a glimpse of Dalt, and he knocked and called his name till Dalt came to the door and let him in.

Dalt gestured, and the police chief sat at the round table there in the common room. Dalt sat nearby at the fireplace. Don noticed at once Dalt was dressed, but he was wearing socks, no shoes, and his clothes were wrinkled. So it looked as if Dalt slept in his clothes last night. And he could understand that, knowing as he did how close Dalt and Sted were.

Yet, he sensed something about Dalt, something new, not sorrowing, but open to new things. Not closed, as he had been on every occasion before when Don spoke with him. There was an openness now. Something was new.

There was a noise from the kitchen, and Don was surprised to hear it. "Is that Nell?" he asked.

"No, it's Lela. I don't know if Nell will ever come back."

"Hello, Lela," Don called out. "You making coffee?"

"Yep."

"Make some for me?" Don had a thin folder with him. He tapped the edge of it against the table top, thinking. *Mighty early for Lela to be here.*

She came with their coffee and some for herself. She made an extra trip for milk and sugar. Don had the opportunity to look her over. Her clothes were also sort of rumpled, and she had no shoes on. Black stockings, no shoes.

Oh, oh. Slept here. With him. With clothes on?

The second time she came to the table, she lingered near Dalt, and then she leaned over him. She kissed the top of his head. "I love this man," she said.

Dalt's face lit up, and his high cheekbones flushed red. *So that's how it is*, Don thought. *One bad thing ending, one good thing just beginning.*

He couldn't help thinking to himself he could win at poker if he played with Dalt, the way those cheekbones turned red. *You have a "tell", Dalt. Don't gamble.*

"You'd better talk to your dog, then," he said dryly.

"He's being quiet this morning," Lela said, "over here, this side of Dalt's chair."

"Planning his evil day," was Dalt's comment.

"Everything is in one place, cars and all, all the evidence anyone could ask for, all right there. The bodies are in bad shape," Don informed them.

"He started taking long walks. I guess he was picking out his perfect spot." Dalt looked at Don with an earnest expression. "He wasn't crazy every minute, every day. He would go for long stretches just the same old Sted. Then he'd have dreams, and that would do it."

"The Stevens boy wasn't there with the others," Don said softly, and, just as he thought would happen, Dalt's body became tense.

For a minute, Dalt was still. Then, he said thoughtfully, "When Sted's aunt was trying to take everything away from him, I was sure, somehow, he was still alive and that he'd need all that if he got home. I never felt so alone. For a while there, Nell was feeding me because she knew how it was. There were times when there would be fog all around this place, and I could have sworn I was on some ship in the middle of a sea and nobody else around for miles. Have you ever felt so alone? That's what it was for me for a long time. Without Sted, this place was crippled."

Don sipped his coffee, taking that in. He knew about being alone. He remembered someone so important to him lashing out, saying, "All you do is analyze, analyze. Don't you ever do anything just because it feels good?" He did the worst thing possible; he ignored the problem.

"I remember Sted dropping by my office. He said he figured the Stevens boy had never taken those anchors. He thought maybe the kid tossed them into the lake somehow, just for meanness. I know some say he's a runaway, but it wouldn't do him much good if he turned up now, would it? His uncle's gone, his mother's gone. Some say she's back in Ohio to live near family. No, I think he drowned in that lake. He was messing around with those anchors, and he couldn't swim; that's the way I see it. I'm closing that case, and even if his body turned up tomorrow, I'd say it was the same thing—accidental drowning. That's what I came to tell you. His case is closed."

They talked a while more about other minor things. He noticed Dalt's body relaxed, and his breathing became regular. *This man was family*, he thought to himself, *not by blood, but by dedication. He would do whatever it took to help Sted. He deserves a break.*

He left the folder on the table when he left them. "Start a fire with that," he said.

When Dalt looked back later, on those years when Sted and he were young, carefree fellows, just arrived at the cottage, he remembered how they would rough-house for the fun of it. "You want to fight?" one or the other would challenge. "I can take you down," they would say, laughing.

"Maybe. Maybe I will," might be the reply. When they tested each other till one would cry uncle, there were never any hurt feelings. Seeing Sted at the foot of those porch steps, holding a gun, the person Dalt saw there was a young Sted. He never saw a murderer. He just saw a friend. Maybe his friend, that youth he felt was his brother, got tired of sometimes being crazy, sometimes normal. Maybe in the war, he was almost able to welcome death, since he was so tired of life.

He and Lela visited Sted in the institution where he was kept. He always recognized and was glad to see Dalt. Ricky, recovered from the gunshot, never went with them to see him. But he was on the porch waiting to hear how their visit went when they got back.

Sometimes Sted confused Lela by touching her hair, asking if she'd dyed it. "He's mixed you up with Faye, I think," Dalt told her.

The last time they saw him, Sted looked tired, and he'd lost weight. "You remember how much fun we had, riding those horses?" Dalt asked him.

"Yeah," Sted smiled and nodded his head.

Shortly after that last visit, Sted died. His body was placed in the New York cemetery where his family was buried: Eva, Helen, Reginald, and Stedman, in that order, graves all in a line. On Mother's Day, Dalt took flowers to put on his mother Mia's grave—his parents were in the same cemetery—and he also put flowers on Helen's grave.

Bill Accardi never had to look for a house. Dalt gave him

land to build on just on the other side of the garden. The cottage was on the town grid, but Bill's house would not be, so this meant putting in a deep well, a septic tank and cesspool. He had electricity from the beginning. He often went whistling through the garden on his way to fish, and his parents did visit. He never remarried.

The angel is still in the garden, but nobody hears Faye singing lullabies. In Nell's church, sweet voices sing, though. Nell continued to work at the cottage for years, but instead of coming by boat, she always arrived in her car. Tim entered college, the first in his family to do so.

The place is now The Conshe Mountain Guest House. Guests can spend the night and have breakfast, or they can stay longer.

Lela and Dalt married one Christmas Eve day in front of the big fireplace in the common room. The cottage was always full of their happiness. Having decided the illuminated Bible had to have been Helen's, they decided to keep it and not sell it. Dalt died in Lela's arms when he was eighty-nine. She died about a year or so later. They chose to be buried at the back of the garden near a hedge of lilacs.

No one remembers anything about the death of Ruben.

For a while, it was Tim and Bill, and Nell ran the place, but it ended up, after Bill and Nell died, becoming just Tim and his family owning it. Tim Junior is thinking of restoring the barn and adding some horses, but presently, he'll take you for a ride to enjoy the fall colors in his electric cart.

Now, this is a post note concerning the first time Lela and Dalt slept together. It was really the second time they were in bed together. They never felt the first time should count because they were clothed and dealing with a very bad time on that first occasion.

This time, she was wearing the top of Dalt's pajamas, and he was wearing the bottoms. He opened a window a bit, even though the night was cold, because he hoped if it were chilly in the room, perhaps she would curl around him as she had the first time, and put one arm over him. The first time when she did that, it filled his heart with pleasure.

There was cuddling, love, sweet whisperings, and then darkness and silence as they were drifting into sleep. Then, suddenly, came Dalt's voice. "Is Ruben sleeping in his bed, Lela? I think he's up on the bed with us. You feel that? I think he's on the bed around my feet. Is he up here with us?"

A pause. Then Lela's voice. "Yes, I can tell that. He's over there by your feet."

"Why *my* feet?"

"Just reach down there and push him off. Or push him off with your foot."

Silence. A long silence.

Then, "Oh. That's all right then. Let's leave him alone."

Was that a giggle? No matter. Lela turned. She curled her body around his back, and she put one arm around him, embracing him.

And then she sighed. It was a deep sigh, and Dalt heard it. Somewhere between a sigh of his own and a smile, he fell asleep.

As for the little white Ruben dog that so comfortably slept at Dalt's big, reliable feet... that dog Nell said spent a good part of every day looking for trouble and the rest of it barking about it... that dog who was faithful only to Lela and sometimes to Dalt... that dog so much like the people of the country where his breed developed, not given to sentiment... did that dog ever, even once in his lifetime, give a grateful sigh of happiness and love?

If he ever did, he kept that to himself.

We must hope his little body rests near Lela, where he always wanted to be.

We shall never know.

The End